What the critics are saying...

৪৩

5 Stars "A Touch of Fae by Lauren Dane is, well, astounding! It has been a while since a book caused me to laugh in excitement and joy until the tears run down my face; but, Ms. Dane accomplished that and more with apparent ease." ~ *Ecataromance*

5 Angels and a Recommended Read! "Ms. Dane has delivered a wonderful story yet again. I cannot wait to hear what happens next in this series. I hope there will be more. This world is too fascinating for the series to be done." ~ *Fallen Angel Reviews*

5 Cups! "Ms. Dane has woven a fantastic story of fantasy and romance tinged with humor. A Touch of Fae is a book that I would read again and again. Good job, Ms. Dane."
~ *Coffeetime Romance*

5 Cupids! "I loved the storyline, the people and foremost—the sexy faerie warrior Con!!!!! The tender behavior of sexy Con, his protective instincts—together with the magic flair of the Faerie-World, all of this together are ingredients for one of the best stories I have read for a couple of months!"
~ *Cupid's Library Reviews*

A Touch
OF Fae

LAUREN DANE

ELLORA'S CAVE
ROMANTICA PUBLISHING

An Ellora's Cave Romantica Publication

www.ellorascave.com

A Touch of Fae

ISBN 1419953974, 9781419953972
ALL RIGHTS RESERVED.
A Touch of Fae Copyright © 2005 Lauren Dane
Edited by Ann Leveille.
Cover art by Niki Browning.

This book printed in the U.S.A. by Jasmine-Jade Enterprises, LLC.

Electronic book Publication August 2005
Trade paperback Publication May 2006

Content Advisory:

S – ENSUOUS
E – ROTIC
X – TREME

Ellora's Cave Publishing offers three levels of Romantica™ reading entertainment: S (S-ensuous), E (E-rotic), and X (X-treme).

The following material contains graphic sexual content meant for mature readers. This story has been rated E–rotic.

S-*ensuous* love scenes are explicit and leave nothing to the imagination.

E-*rotic* love scenes are explicit, leave nothing to the imagination, and are high in volume per the overall word count. E-rated titles might contain material that some readers find objectionable—in other words, almost anything goes, sexually. E-rated titles are the most graphic titles we carry in terms of both sexual language and descriptiveness in these works of literature.

X-*treme* titles differ from E-rated titles only in plot premise and storyline execution. Stories designated with the letter X tend to contain difficult or controversial subject matter not for the faint of heart.

Also by Lauren Dane

ം

About the Author

෨

Lauren Dane been writing stories since she was able to use a pencil, and before that she used to tell them to people. Of course, she still talks nonstop, but now she decided to try and make a go of being a writer. And so here she is. She still loves to write, and through wonderful fate and good fortune, she's able to share what she writes with others now. It's a wonderful life!

The basics: She's a mom, a partner, a best friend and a daughter. Living in the rainy but beautiful Pacific Northwest, she spends her late evenings writing like a fiend when she finally wrestles all of her kids to bed.

Lauren welcomes comments from readers. You can find her website and email address on her author bio page at www.ellorascave.com.

Tell Us What You Think

We appreciate hearing reader opinions about our books. You can email us at Comments@EllorasCave.com.

Irish Gaelic Words

ഔ

Gaelic is an old and very beautiful language. As I wrote this book and I learned more of it, the more romantic I realized it was. The pronunciation is a bit difficult for me, but as Con used so many of these phrases with Em, I thought it might be helpful to include a short dictionary of the Gaelic terms and a close approximation of their pronunciation where I was able to find it:

A Ghra (ah hraw) – my love

A Thaisce (ah hash-keh) – my treasure

Tá mo chroí istigh ionat go deo – my heart is in you forever

Mo Fiach – my raven

A Ghrá mo Chroí (ah hraw muh hree) – my Heart's Beloved

Is tusa mo shaol – You are my world (as in life)

Namhaid – enemy

Fear cheile – husband

Bean cheile – wife

A TOUCH OF FAE

�’၅၁

Dedication

As always, for Ray, who loves me even when I'm grumpy and editing. For my children, who help me appreciate the wonder of the magic in the world. Mom and Dad, even though I cringe at the thought that you may actually read my books, I'd be lost without all the support you give me.

Special thanks go to the fabulous ladies in my Yahoo loop who keep me writing with their excellent feedback and encouragement. To my ever so wonderful beta readers who never pull punches just to get free hot sexy stories — Di, Julia and Tracy — my books are better because of your input.

Sparkles and Piston, how can I express how important your friendship is to me? Having people who are where you are and get what you're going through and who also have great talent and insight is such a blessing. Oh, and all of the giggling is just icing.

And last but not least, Ann, my own personal grammar goddess — thank you.

Trademarks Acknowledgement

≈

The author acknowledges the trademarked status and trademark owners of the following wordmarks mentioned in this work of fiction:

Guardian: Guardian Newspaper Limited
Gucci: Gucci America, Inc.
Hermès Paris: Hermès International
Jacuzzi: Jacuzzi, Inc.Kate Spade: Kate Spade, LLC
Leisure Suit Larry: Sierra Entertainment, Inc.
Prada: Prefel S.A. Corporation

Chapter One

❧

Em Charvez hurried along Pirate's Alley toward The Grove, her family's shop. It was January and the brightly colored walls and doors of the narrow passage greeted her as she held her coat closed against the wind and the rain. The drops fell sideways in icy missiles, pelting her already chilled skin, stinging her face and hands. She cursed herself for forgetting an umbrella, although in this kind of weather it would have blown inside out anyway.

Minutes before, as the storm approached on the wind, she'd stood on the banks of the river staring at the white froth of the waves and the steel gray hue of the water. The water could be muddy, green or that gray-blue. The river had always held a deep fascination for her and she often came to walk the Moonwalk when she needed to think about things.

Hoping to beat the storm but wanting to warm up she'd stopped at Café Du Monde for a café au lait and a bag of beignets on her way to the shop. Just as she'd crossed the street and entered Jackson Square the rain had started and she hurried along as best she could, knowing that she'd be soaked by the time she got to work.

Her heart began to lighten as she approached the block that held The Grove. She walked through the front door. The jingling of the chimes and the scents of the oils and herbs assailed her and calmed her frustration at having to leave the research she'd been doing with the books and papers she brought back from Chicago.

The shop held all manner of magical items as well as healing herbs and teas, special aromatic candles and oils and readings done by her *grandmere* and her *tante* Lou. More than any other place, it was her spiritual home.

"Hey! How are you?" her sister Lee called out.

"Wet and cold. But I did bring you something." She dropped the bag with the still-hot beignets on the counter.

"Oh! Thank you, Em! My favorite." Her sister dug into the bag, pulling out the sweet dough confection and eating it, getting grease and powdered sugar everywhere in the process.

Em laughed as she hung up her coat and caught the towel her *grandmere* tossed her way to dry her hair off with.

"So tell me already, little raven. I can see how excited you are," her *grandmere* said as Em took a long drink of the chicory-flavored coffee and sighed with satisfied pleasure as the heat coursed through her system.

Em smiled at the use of her childhood nickname. "You know me too well, *Grandmere*. I've found something interesting in some of the books and papers from Alex's grandfather's collection. I have this *feeling* that the demon lord isn't done with us, with trying to break the Compact. It's all a matter of how. So I've been keeping an eye out in my research and well, I've found something." Her *grandmere* sighed and nodded in agreement. Em pulled out a sheet that she'd photocopied before she left Chicago the week before. "This passage refers to some ancient text on chaotic magic, there's this sketch in the margin." Em picked up a pen and sketched a facsimile of the faint drawing on a separate piece of paper. "Have you ever seen this?" she asked.

The older woman looked at the group of odd runic symbols carefully, tracing them thoughtfully with a fingertip. "No, but this seems familiar."

That had been niggling at her, she could almost feel what the symbol meant but she couldn't quite grasp it. It kept eluding her and she was frustrated. She was glad she wasn't the only one. "It does, doesn't it? Well, anyway," she folded up the paper, put it back into her bag and tossed it into a chair, "I have so much more of the Carter Collection to catalog and go through. I can't believe how wonderful Alex is being over this."

Lee hugged her sister tightly. "Alex is a great guy, isn't he? He knows how much you love books and the idea of being the first on the path of light to read some of those ancient dark magic texts. You know how hesitant he was to take anything from his grandfather at first. If it wasn't for you talking with him about the historical importance of the collection, who knows where it would have ended up. So of course he's only too happy to let you at them first."

"Well, still, I know that others have asked to see the collection but that he's put them off until I'm done. It's a very sweet thing for him to do."

Lee shrugged with a smile. "You know that Alex wants you to be the curator of the collection and you know that you're more than qualified for the job. Alex will let other people view the collection but as far as he's concerned, it's your decision as to how and when that happens."

Lee watched the flush of pleasure come over Em's face at the compliment. Lee loved her sister very much but she didn't always understand her. Eric was Lee's twin brother and they had an unspoken rapport that she wished she had with her sister. She wasn't empathic like Em was, but she could tell that something was wrong, that Em seemed unhappy and a bit melancholy. Over the last year, especially over the last six months since Lee's wedding and the vanquishing of the dark mage in Chicago, her sister had felt more and more distant.

Truth was, Lee was more than a bit jealous of Alex. He seemed to understand her sister better than she did. The two of them seemed to really strike a chord with books and magic and research and Alex connected with Em in a way that she wished she could. Em and Alex had talked of nothing but those books for the last month. More often than not when Em called or stopped by it was to talk to Alex instead of her.

Seeing the distance and the dissatisfaction grow, Lee had tried to talk to Em about it several times. But Em just changed the subject and Lee didn't want to push. She only hoped the research made her happier. If things didn't resolve themselves soon, Lee would push her sister into a confrontation to work it all out as a family.

* * * * *

On Tir na nOg, the queen raised her head at the moment Em sketched the symbol on that paper, the echo of Isolde tracing it with a finger wrapping around her consciousness. Alarmed, she quickly stood up and went to her scrying bowl. She poured water into it and waved her hand over the surface, speaking the words of the spell that would allow her to see through the Veil that separated the world of Fae from the human world.

The face of a raven-haired woman with big green eyes shimmered to the surface. She had almost delicate features but a determined chin. Aine looked at her and saw the sadness resonating from her. She listened to the woman speaking with the elder human and, with a small frown, spoke out a name in summons.

Moments later a tall warrior with hair the color of caramel walked into the room and bowed low before her. His hair was long and it slid over his shoulders as he did so, the braids at his temples swaying slightly. His muscles rippled as he stood straight again, his golden eyes flared with intelligence and mischief.

"Conchobar, I need you," Aine announced as she smoothed her skirts and sat down on her bed.

At that, a sexy smile slowly slid across his lips. "Is that so, my queen? It has been two thousand years since I last warmed your bed but I would be most happy to do my duty now."

She stifled a smile at his irrepressible nature. "I need you to cross the Veil and keep an eye on a human for me."

His only answer was a raised brow.

"She wrote one of the symbols of the first books of the Tuatha De Danann. More specifically, I believe it is from *Crossing the Veil.*"

His face went from sexy boredom to acute interest.

Aine gave a satisfied smirk and raised a brow. "Yes, I thought you might be interested. I don't know who this woman is or what she knows but apparently she's got some knowledge and I need to know just how much so I can proceed."

"Just watch her? Why don't I bring her back here to speak to you? If she has the book she could unleash forces beyond her control." He had a hard time stifling the look of irritation on his face. He was too damned old to be put on babysitting watch over some human.

"Yes, just watch her and keep me apprised of what she's up to. Do not make contact with her and keep your glamour, I do not want her to know of our existence. She doesn't know what the symbol means nor does she know where it comes from. I do not want to bring her over unless it's absolutely necessary."

"As you wish, my queen," Con said and bowed before he left her.

* * * * *

Conchobar MacNessa walked out of the room and stalked down the long hallway to the quarters of the Favored. Many women of the Court tried to catch his eye as he passed but failed. Con had work on his mind and, as much as he admired the female form, he was focused on the task at hand.

As one of the oldest and most revered of the Queen's Favored, he was a fierce warrior, a brilliant tactician and a trusted councilor. At ten thousand years old, he had battled through the last major war between the Fae and the Dark Fae.

His reputation had taken on mythic proportions but most of it was true.

When he entered the main chamber, many of the younger Fae there straightened, standing taller, thrusting out their chests as if merely by his presence, he'd ordered them to stand at attention. He gave a casual wave of his hand as he walked through the room toward a red-haired warrior seated at a large table, cleaning a long-handled knife.

He sat down and a mug of steaming tea appeared quickly near his hand, deposited by one of the more eager apprentices. Con smiled and nodded his head in thanks at the younger Fae and looked back to the other man.

"So, I'm off to the other side," he said simply.

Jayce MacTavish raised a fiery eyebrow and waited for Con to tell him the details.

"Seems a human female may have something of ours." He didn't go into specifics about the book, he was in a room with many other people and he didn't want to broadcast that there were Books out there among humans.

Jayce picked up on the seriousness in Con's voice and continued to polish the knife. "Need any help?"

"No, it should be simple enough. Probably a total waste of time." The annoyance in his voice at having to baby-sit a human was clear and Jayce snorted with humor.

"How long?"

Con shrugged. "As long as she wills it," he said, referring to Aine.

"Better you than me. You will let me know if you need anything, won't you?" He gave his best friend a glare.

Con made a noncommittal sound and Jayce sighed.

"Well, at least there'll be more women for the rest of us with you gone," Jayce said, knowing that if it truly got bad Con would come to him but also knowing that his friend was very overprotective of those he cared about and would take a lot onto his own shoulders before he'd ever put anyone else in danger.

"Only until I come back. It must be hard for you, Jayce my man, to know that while you're swiving them, they're calling out my name." Con chuckled and avoided Jayce's lazy swipe with his fist. His face turned serious. "You will keep an eye out, yes?"

Jayce sobered as well. "I will. You know I am as uncomfortable as you are with this new information about the Dark Fae. I don't trust their motives, Con."

"Aye, me neither. But we can't turn our backs on them. We don't know how big of at threat they pose or their numbers. But we do know that MacAillen is involved and as the humans say, the apple doesn't fall far from the tree. Come to me should a problem arise."

Jayce nodded solemnly and Con stood, touched his forehead, made his farewells and shimmered out of the room.

Con found himself standing in his home on the shores of the Western Seas. He didn't need much but he wanted to check on his dog, who would be with his brother Finn while he was on the other side, not knowing how long he'd be there. Except for the dog, Con lived as a solitary man. His bed was never cold for very long, but his heart remained untouched by any woman who wasn't related to him. He left the romanticism to his brother.

Con was the kind of warrior whose blade was always razor-sharp but who preferred negotiation to battle. His muscles were hard and tightened by work. He spent his time these days with Jayce, training those new warriors who sought the honor of the Favored.

Behind the mischievous glint in his eyes, there was a certain loneliness, a pain that was only very rarely visible. Only three people in the world knew that he didn't let people get close because he felt he'd failed his father several thousand years before. He hid that vulnerability with a devil-may-care attitude and an endless line of women, none of whom could ever hold his heart.

* * * * *

Early April saw Em strolling through Spanish Plaza and taking in the Lundi Gras crowds. In a few minutes it would be six and Rex would be arriving, marking the official start of Mardi Gras. Being a local, it was a favorite time of year. The tourists were there but Lundi Gras was more of an event for the locals. Of course in these few days' time the area would be swollen with tourists there to celebrate Mardi Gras, the shop would do the biggest business of the year and afterwards they'd all take a few days off.

She was on the arm of Jon Boudreaux, an old friend of the family and her date for the day. She'd really tried to get excited about him, he was handsome and well mannered, and he already knew that she was a feeler and could pick up thoughts and emotions from others and he was okay with that. She knew he liked her and was sexually attracted to her even though she tried to keep her gift turned way down when she was with other people in social situations. That was one of the problems with being an empath. She picked up on other people's emotions and motivations all the time—it was like constant background noise.

No, truth was she just saw him like the cousin he reminded her of. She was troubled by the whole state of her life, though. She was a twenty-five-year-old woman in one of the most fun cities in the world and she was still a virgin. She got asked on dates pretty often but she rarely accepted. When you could pick up a guy's intention to fuck you and move on, or his acute discomfort with your being a witch or the fact that he wondered why you weren't as hot as your sister, well, it just tended to make one very picky.

But the heart of the matter was that Em was very unhappy with the current state of her life. She felt like she was living in the shadow of the other strong women in her life, she felt weighed down by her virginity, by being the bookishly quiet one in a family of boisterous extroverts. Worse, by her family's inability to see her as anything other than "shy, bookish Em" when she wasn't that person at all, not really. She was tempted to just sleep with Jon to be rid of her bothersome hymen and break free of the stereotype her family's perception, but couldn't really bring herself to endorse the idea.

She looked at his profile. He was a truly handsome man. She loved the sharpness of his cheekbones and the dimple in his chin. She tried to will herself into sexual interest but when she thought of them in bed together she wanted to laugh. Surely not a good sign.

Thing was, she'd dreamed of one man her whole life. He was tall and broad with the chest and arms of a warrior. He had golden skin and hair that wasn't quite blond, wasn't quite brown with a bit of copper thrown in. It was long and flowing with braids at his temples and he had eyes that were gold, sometimes the color of whiskey. He'd taken her in every way imaginable and a few she'd never even thought of.

Thinking of her dream man had made her achy and her panties wet. He was the star of every sexual fantasy she'd ever had — she'd never had an orgasm without his face on her mind. She sighed wistfully and shifted her attention back to the present.

As they moved closer to the stage at the end of the Plaza to hear the jazz band, she bumped into someone and looked up, smiling. "Excuse me," she called out with a laugh. It wasn't like you didn't run into a hundred people on a day like Lundi Gras.

A pair of blue-gray eyes blinked down at her, mischief twinkling in them. "Of course," he said with a slight accent. Irish, she thought. He winked and kept on moving and she couldn't resist a quick look over her shoulder at his retreating form. He had quite a nice behind. She smiled and turned back to the stage.

Con kept his sexy smile as he walked away. He knew he shouldn't have come close to her, she was a witch after all, but he had to touch her, smell her, have her look at him. After seeing her daily for the last three months he'd become fascinated with Emily Charvez. More than fascinated — he lusted after her like a panting dog. There was something about her sweet manner, her genuineness that touched him, turned him on.

He'd watched her as she worked in her family's magic shop, watched her cook dinner in her tiny apartment, followed her as she browsed the French Market and the shops for spices and oils. He was enamored of the way she went to Café Du Monde every Friday morning and had a café au lait and three beignets. He remembered the first time he'd watched as she licked the powdered sugar from her bottom lip. She had a nearly feline sensuality about her and yet she didn't seem to know it. This only made her appeal to him more.

He loved it when she sat in a sunny window and worked with her books. The light showed the blue-black of her hair, hair as black as a raven's wing. Her skin was like milk. There were times when he simply could not help himself and he had to get close enough to her to breathe her in. She smelled so good to him.

Yes, his feelings about Em Charvez had gone from annoyance to near obsession in those months he watched her and it certainly hadn't helped that he found it necessary to peek in on her when she took a shower or was sleeping. After she'd gone in the mornings, he took a moment to put his face into her pillow and inhale deeply, pulling her scent into his senses where he could hold her all day.

He really hoped that this whole issue of the book came to nothing so that his queen wouldn't want her dead and he could pursue the raven-haired beauty for himself and his bed.

Con eyed the man with her narrowly. He'd scented her desire as he'd passed and now he fought a rising tide of annoyance. The cream trickling from her pussy should be his.

Would be his. He itched to give the man a rash or a stomach ailment but held back. If Aine found out he'd done such a thing she'd be angry, they weren't supposed to harm humans. Pouting, Con kept walking and kept his curses to himself.

* * * * *

Em sat, staring at the pages on the desk in front of her. She shook her head and read the passages again. A frown marred her features as she sat back with a concerned sigh. It wasn't quite summer yet but the already oppressive heat pressed against the windows and she knew that her weak air conditioner would only be effective for another few weeks. She took a few long drinks of her iced tea and doodled as she thought over what she'd been reading.

If what she had found was correct, it could spell trouble for those who used magic to protect innocents and more specifically, the Compact that the Charvez witches were bound by. A Compact she'd only been told about the year before and had been endlessly fascinated with.

She'd spent the last five months researching the one passage she'd found in the journal of a twelfth-century death wielder about a book that contained the key to using two opposing forces to dissolve any magical agreements or bonds. By her loose translation of the Latin and bastardized Greek, she thought the book was called *The Shifting Veil*. She couldn't be sure, there was another language there, one that she'd never seen before. It was mainly dominated by runic symbols but she felt that she understood it on some subconscious level.

It had been that way forever. She intuitively understood things related to magic—she didn't always have a perfect grasp and it wasn't always clear—but if she just let go a bit, things would sometimes just come to her. It's what made her such a great researcher, she just followed her gut.

Over the last five months, Em's biggest challenge had been to figure out where all of the references had come from. She had traced some of the text to a collection of extremely rare books. Of course she'd traced them to several possible places and most of those leads had proven fruitless. However, a few days prior, she'd found out that a collector of arcane magical texts had died sixty years before. The books from his library had been sold at an auction. She had a feeling she knew who might have purchased them there.

Deciding to go with that hunch, Em pulled out her address book, flipped it open and grabbed the telephone.

A richly accented voice answered. "Yes, hello?"

"Mrs. Belton? This is Emily Charvez from New Orleans."

"Oh, Em! How nice to hear from you again. It's been a long time. Since that last call we had, what was it? Two years ago? My, you're really turning heads out there in the magical community. I was quite impressed with your last paper. You're making quite a name for yourself as an eminent authority on magical research."

Em laughed, a pleased blush creeping up her neck. "Well, I don't know that I'd go that far but I do like to research and I love books. In fact, that's what I was calling about. I was wondering, is your offer to talk with me about your collection still open? I'm going to be in London in a few weeks and I'd appreciate the chance to speak with you about your library. I'd love to talk about some rare books with you over dinner. My treat."

"Oh of course! As a fellow book lover you should know I'd never be able to turn down a chance to talk about them with you, especially over a free meal. And I love to show my books off to people who can truly appreciate them," the older witch said with a laugh.

They ironed out a few more details and Em hung up. Adelade Belton was one of the foremost magical scholars in the world and her library was the most comprehensive. Em had a feeling that some of those books had ended up in Adelade Belton's library. Em had been itching to see it for years now and it seemed like she'd finally get the chance.

Chapter Two

Emily Charvez looked out the window of the airplane as it approached Heathrow for landing. She smiled, it was her first trip out of the United States and she was going alone. Her smile lessened a bit as she thought of how her family had urged her to take one of them along. She'd argued vigorously that she'd wanted to do it on her own. She was twenty-five years old and totally capable of traveling to England to track down some rare magical texts without a brother in tow, thank you very much! She felt a little like a magical Nancy Drew.

The worst thing had been that Lee had taken their mother's side. She'd insisted that Em should take an escort even though Em knew good and well that Lee would have made the trip alone without batting an eye. Em sighed at another example of how everyone saw her as helpless and shy while they saw Lee as a freaking superhero.

In the end, she'd agreed to stay in one of Aidan's boutique hotels in London and to call daily as the price of being left alone to make the trip on her own. A small price to pay really, she knew Aidan's hotels had to be pretty darned nice and it saved her some major cash.

The flight attendants came by to take trash and prepare everyone for landing and she put away her journal and sat back.

"You'll be sure to give me a telephone call, then?" the woman next to Em asked her.

"Of course, you've been so lovely. I do hope you'll let me take you to lunch." Em smiled at the elderly woman sitting next to her. Figures, the cute guy who'd been making eyes at her back at La Guardia had a seat a few rows back and she'd noticed with a sigh that the young woman who sat next to him had already worked hard at catching that eye. Just her luck that she'd ended up next to the older woman who spent the entire flight from New York talking about her dogs and her son the dentist.

"Oh please do! You must come by my home for tea, perhaps my son will be around," her elderly seatmate said with a bright smile.

Em smiled back. She'd picked up that the woman desperately wanted to see her son married and with a family before she died. She'd also picked up that this son may not be playing on her team and his mother was a bit concerned about his "friend", who her son seemed to be so close to.

After the plane landed, Em headed to the immigration checkpoint and sweet deluded Mrs. Eddington went to get her bags.

Once she'd cleared immigration and claimed her bags, Em was happily surprised to see that Aidan had arranged for a car to pick her up and take her to the hotel. On the way into the city, she called back home. She and Lee had come to a truce after the arguments about her traveling alone and Lee was treading carefully to keep things smooth. Em had the distinct feeling that Alex was behind that.

"Hello?" her sister's voice rang out.

"Lee, I just wanted to call to say I got in all right and to thank Aidan for the car."

"He's sleeping but I'll tell him when he wakes up. You know how he worries. He's arranged for a suite for you at the hotel, don't argue or call and complain and don't try to get into another room. He won't have it and as he owns the damned place, they won't move you even if you ask."

"Lee!"

"What? He loves you, it's his hotel, he likes to spoil the women in his life. What can I say? Other than thank god he's all mine!" She giggled. "Seriously, *cher*, just enjoy it and order loads of room service."

Em sighed but smiled. "Tell him thank you, I'll try to call when it's dark there so I can tell him myself. You take care and I'll see you in two weeks."

"I will and you too, okay? Call me at least every day or I'll call you. I love you, Em. Have fun. If you need me you'll call, won't you? I'm here for you, you know that, right?"

She knew they were all worried about her and she felt guilty but then it pissed her off that she felt guilty over getting her own life in order. She shook it off, she was a continent away from them and she'd damn well fix what ailed her on her own.

"I do know that and I appreciate it. I love you for it. I'll talk to you soon, please tell *Maman* and *Papa* that I arrived safely," she said just before she hung up.

* * * * *

The doorman helped her out of the car and escorted her inside. Walking into the beautiful lobby, she tried not to gape in awe. The place was gorgeous and classy. Clearly a lot of money had been spent to decorate. Rather than appear garish the small hotel had an understated old-world charm.

Still in a state of pleased surprise at her surroundings, the doorman handed Em off to the manager, coming out from behind a rather ornate wooden counter. He took her hand with a smile.

"Ms. Charvez, welcome to London and the Belleville. The driver called ahead to let us know you were on your way and everything is ready for you. Mr. Bell wants you to know that if you have need of anything, all that is required is for you to but ask. The Belleville has a twenty-four-hour concierge ready to meet any need you may have." He motioned to the bellman, who placed her suitcases on a cart and escorted her to the elevator.

When it went all the way to the top floor she held her breath with anticipation about what the place would look like. As the doors slid open she wasn't disappointed.

"Uh, I was under the impression I was staying in a suite," she said, stunned by the massive penthouse apartment with huge windows overlooking the city in three directions.

"These are Mr. Bell and Ms. Charvez's personal apartments. He wanted to be sure you stayed here. The kitchen is fully stocked and someone will arrive tomorrow morning to bring your breakfast. A cook is also available for other meals should you desire it. Simply use the phone to call down and request it. You may also request a car for any transportation needs," the bellman said, politely ignoring the look of shock on Em's face.

She reached into her bag to tip him but he shook his head. "No, Ms. Charvez, no need to tip any of us on your visit, it's all been taken care of. Please enjoy your stay." He started toward the elevators. "If you set this lock here, the elevators will not be able to open without a key card. If you need someone to unpack your clothing or press anything, just call downstairs."

After he left she wandered the penthouse. Damn, it sure did pay to know the rich and privileged. She chose the master suite, which had a large bed that sat in the middle of the room. She opened the doors, walked out onto the terrace and gazed out over the Thames River and London Bridge.

Emily Charvez was looking for something.

All her life she'd been different from most people, and that served to keep her close to her family and the women who shared her differences. She could feel when people were lying or insincere, she could tell when someone didn't like her or wanted to cause her or someone else harm.

It was difficult to make friends because she could read when people were scared by her gift or if they wanted her to use it as a parlor trick or other, worse things. So she stuck with family. She had many cousins who were near her age and she had Lee. They were all different, and in that difference they were the same.

In most ways, Lee was her best friend as well as her sister. At the same time, Em grew up in Lee's shadow. Lee was their mother's favorite, Lee was the witch dreamer, the most powerful Charvez of their generation and the most powerful witch dreamer in seven generations. She was bold and smart and independent. Em was the quiet one. Where Lee had gorgeous, long, curly auburn hair and lavender eyes, Em had close-cropped hair as dark as night and green eyes. Lee was petite and fecund and Em was tall and, well, she was long and lean but she was blessed in the boob department. She got that from their mother. While Lee looked like a doll, men were usually put off by Em's height. Just once Em wanted to feel dainty when with a man.

Em realized that she needed this time away from her family to figure out what her next step in life was going to be. She was a twenty-five-year-old virgin witch who loved books and lived inside her head. She needed to live a little, to do it away from the notorious Charvez women and their protective fathers, brothers and cousins. Because, really, she wasn't so much the shy one but the misunderstood one. Em knew she had it in her to be fearless and sexy and she planned to show that to everyone else too.

With a smile of resolve, she wandered back inside and unpacked her things. Grabbing a glass of very nice cabernet she went to the terrace outside the living room and sat, watching the city move from late afternoon into evening, doing nothing more than writing in her journal and listening to music, free from worries for the first time in a long while.

She was excited and awestruck. The penthouse was so lavish, it must be what it felt like to be royalty. She grinned, thinking of how fortunate her sister was on all counts. Not just one great guy but two of them. Her painting career was thriving, as was Aidan's. Alex, her other man, was one of New Orleans' most successful financial planners. They had a great house and a great life and they traveled and apparently did it in great style. If she didn't love Lee so much she'd hate her.

Her smile dimmed. It wasn't as if Lee's life was carefree, she'd had to battle an evil dark mage, had watched their great-aunt's murder and had been kidnapped and had her life and the lives of her husbands threatened. Lee deserved her life and her happiness, Em just wanted some for herself.

So, she turned her power down as low as she could so that she wouldn't drown in everyone else's feelings and thoughts, changed her clothes and washed her face and headed out to grab a bite.

* * * * *

After he'd assured himself of Em's safety at the restaurant, Con knew he could avoid it no longer and slipped through the Veil and went directly to the queen.

Aine looked at him with a raised brow. "Con, it's been several weeks since your last report on the human. I was getting ready to send Jayce after you."

He hadn't wanted to leave Em. It wasn't so much that she was weak or fragile—for a human she was very strong—but she was a human and there were dark forces at work and he had grown more attached to her as the months had passed. He was hesitant to let her out of his protection. Knowing time passed differently in Tir na nOg, he also wanted to get back to her as soon as possible, so he launched directly into an explanation.

"She is in London and will try to meet with a human witch who may have the book in her possession. This Emily Charvez does not have the book, as I told you some months back. She is not an evil human. She does not seek the book for her own glory. She is concerned about the innocents her family is bound to protect. A demon lord is involved in attempts to dissolve a Compact that was wrought by Freya," Con explained.

"Why, Conchobar MacNessa, I do get the feeling that you are growing attached to this human female. How long has it been that you've been watching?" This did not sound like his usual banter regarding women. Aine was amused and a bit worried as well.

He tried not to meet her eyes but it was a losing battle, she was on to him. "It has been six months in their time. And she is an admirable person, especially for a human. I do not wish her to be harmed in this. There is something else here at work, something dark."

The Queen pursed her lovely lips and thought about the situation. She'd heard the slight tremor in his voice when he'd spoken of the human woman being harmed. She knew of his feelings of failure regarding his father and although she knew them to be inaccurate, she also knew that guilt didn't work by logic. She could only trust Con's superior judgment and send out a wish to the fates that the situation did not end up harming her friend and councilor.

She made her choice and nodded at him. "Make contact with the human, Con. Do not tell her what you are but get her to involve you in the search. You will be able to guide her in the right direction while you keep me apprised of the situation."

Triumphant, Con hid his predatory smile and bowed to the Queen and left quickly.

* * * * *

The next day Em sat down to a lovely breakfast on the terrace while reading a fashion magazine. She had some scholarly business to attend to and would be meeting with Mrs. Belton about the ancient magical text later that evening but for the rest of the day she planned to shop and be frivolous. It would be the first step in letting the outside Em reflect the inside Em.

To do so, she ordered a car and headed out. Saving quite a pretty penny on her hotel bill had left her with a windfall and she wanted to splurge. She bought a cashmere sweater for Aidan, a silk scarf at Hermès for Lee and a tie and suspender set for Alex. She'd picked up things for everyone else and handed off the packages to the driver, who placed them in the trunk, or rather the boot, of the car when she realized that she hadn't bought herself anything yet.

Three hours later she arrived back at the hotel and sat in the bedroom of the penthouse and slid her hands over the purchases she'd made that afternoon—silk panties, lacy bras, a pair of knee-high, stiletto-heeled leather boots that she'd had to have the moment she spied them in the window, the short skirt that landed mid-thigh, several lovely blouses and a few cashmere sweaters of her own. And the silver hoop earrings that had called to her when she was shopping through an outdoor market.

She napped and got up, showered and got ready. She decided to wear the sexy boots and skirt with a blood-red cashmere sweater. After all, they were gorgeous and she was going to be out, even if it was just a dinner with another scholar.

While waiting in the lobby she began to feel silly for putting on the bright red lipstick before she'd come downstairs. It had been a last-minute lark, her lips were red and shiny and, she thought, pretty sexy against her pale skin and dark hair. Then again, she was a bit put off by looking sexy and it made her nervous that she'd picked up some pretty racy feelings from the bellman and the concierge when she'd come into the lobby.

She was clenching her hands in her lap and had just about talked herself into going into the restroom to take the lipstick off when she saw a small, birdlike woman with short blonde hair and big blue eyes behind gigantic glasses walk into the lobby. Right away Em could feel the other woman's power and knew she was a witch too. It had to be Adelade Belton.

The woman was probably in her early eighties but she looked to be about fifty and she carried herself with confidence. Em liked that.

She stood and walked toward the other woman with a hesitant smile, one you give someone just before you ask if you know them. Beneath that, the two witches sized each other up. Em picked up wariness from her, a bit of admiration, even a bit of fear. She liked the lipstick and the boots.

Em felt better then and gave a wave in greeting. "Hello, Mrs. Belton?" The woman nodded and held out her hands to Em. "It's lovely to see you, to meet you at last after we've spoken so many times," Em said, clasping hands with the other woman.

"You too, dear. I hope you're hungry, the restaurant is only a few blocks away and we can talk about the books while we eat," she said with a smile.

They walked out onto the sidewalk. Em breathed in the air. Every city had a distinctive smell and she was coming to love London's mix of river, exhaust and food stalls. As they began to walk she turned to Mrs. Belton. "London is such a lovely city. I can't believe I don't…"

The air was knocked out of her and she stumbled as she collided with someone. She looked up and into the face of an extraordinarily handsome man with caramel-colored hair that just began to brush the collar of the fisherman's sweater he had on. He gave her a sexy smile and steadied her with large hands.

"Oh, pardon me," he said, still wearing that smile. Her stomach tightened, her nipples hardened and suddenly her silky panties felt tight and wet as her pussy bloomed. She gazed into his honey-brown eyes and felt as if she were falling.

"Are you all right, dear?" Mrs. Belton asked.

Em had to clear her throat twice before any sound could come out. "Yes, yes of course. Please excuse me, I wasn't looking where I was walking," she said to the gorgeous hunk of man candy in front of her. She wanted to giggle once she thought that but held back.

"It was my fault entirely. Can I treat you two ladies to dinner to make up for my appalling behavior?" His voice carried a soft Irish accent.

Em had to physically step back to fight the urge to bury her face in his sweater and breathe him in. This is what became of being a twenty-five-year-old virgin, she thought to herself, you start having to fight the urge to bury your face in the sweaters of strange men you bump into on the street.

"Oh please don't worry about it. I'm fine," Em said, proud that she'd kept her face away from his sweater and hadn't sounded like a bad Marilyn Monroe imitation. She looked to the other woman. "Shall we get going now?"

"Wait," he said and she stood rooted to the spot. "What's your name?"

"I'm Emily, Em Charvez," she said softly, without even planning to.

He took her hand and kissed it. "Em, I'm so pleased to meet you. I'm Con, Con MacNessa."

"Pleased to meet you, too."

"Dinner?"

"Oh, well, I… That is, we, Mrs. Belton and I, are…" Good heavens, could she sound any more witless? This man simply took away her ability to think clearly. She took a deep breath. "I'm afraid that Mrs. Belton and I are going to be discussing business," she finished.

"Ah, I see. Well then, perhaps an after-dinner drink, Em? I really must tell you I don't plan to give up until you agree." He gave a charming smile.

"Doesn't that sound nice? You two young people should most definitely have a drink after dinner. Con, we are eating at The Oak Room, we should be done in two hours." Mrs. Belton wore a small smile as she watched the two young people together. She waved at Con as she drew a speechless Em along with her.

* * * * *

Con stood as he watched Emily walk away on those fuck-me heels. "Jaysus," he breathed out. Just a brush against her, the smell of her skin, the shiny red lips, and his body was on fire, his blood was singing, coursing through his body, his cock hard and pressing against the zipper of his jeans.

As sure as he'd ever been of anything in the ten thousand years he'd been alive, he knew that lithe, sexy Em was meant to be his woman. He leaned back against the wall and ran his fingers through his hair and had to ignore the women who slowed as they walked past and gave him blatant looks, looks of invitation. He smiled to himself, there'd be no more of that. He'd laughed when his brother had told him that when he met his wife all other women ceased to appeal to him. Con knew Magda and loved her—she was a fetching woman, a woman of great power—but he hadn't been able to imagine that any woman would be good enough to make him stop finding other women to fill his bed. He gave a wry smile. It looked as if he were going to have to eat those words. He'd also have to deal with the fact that he'd just lost his heart after guarding it so closely the last several thousand years.

Con loved women. He'd spent millennia bedding them, seducing them, bringing them pleasure as he took his own. Females of every type, human, Faerie, vampire, he'd even had a shapeshifter or two, it didn't matter, he loved them all. Loved the way they tasted, how their skin felt. He loved the little sounds of pleasure they made, the way their power felt. But when compared to his sultry Em, all of those other women seemed flat, colorless. Her wide, hazel green eyes, those long lashes, her creamy skin. He loved her hair. He didn't usually like short hair on women but hers looked tousled, like she'd just rolled out of bed. Her breasts were full, at least a C cup, but the rest of her was long and lean, athletic. He wanted those legs wrapped around his waist as he thrust his cock deep into her pussy, her lips open to receive his kisses, his hands on her breasts, palming her nipples.

He whistled as he headed to The Belleville, where he'd called ahead and had a suite readied. Apparently the penthouse was in use, a friend of Aidan's no doubt, but a suite would do just fine. He hadn't seen his friend the vampire in at least fifty years but he'd heard through the grapevine that he'd recently found his mate. Small world.

* * * * *

Once they were seated in the restaurant and had ordered, Em and Adelade—she'd been ordered to call the older woman by her first name—got down to business.

"I sense that this visit is more than just a basic information request about my library," Adelade said.

Em smiled. "You're right, I didn't want to talk about it over the phone and I'm not sure this public a venue is the best place either."

Adelade looked concerned but moved her wrist and said something under her breath and the sounds of the room faded. "I've invoked a privacy spell."

"Well, you know that we are the Compact holders in New Orleans?"

"Yes. I understand your sister had quite a job on her hands defending against a dark mage last year. I'm sorry you lost Elise, she was an amazing woman," Adelade said softly. Adelade had been friends with Em's great-aunt for thirty years. The witch dreamer had come to her several times for help with research and other matters regarding the magical world's governance over the years. Elise had also used Adelade's connections to make diplomatic arrangements when she needed to deal with other magical families and organizations for one reason or another. When Adelade had gotten the news that a dark mage had murdered Elise it had sent her reeling and she was certain that the rest of the Charvez family felt her absence quite keenly.

Em blinked back tears, thinking of the great-aunt she'd loved so much. "Thank you. I know you and she were friends, it meant a lot to us to get your letter. We don't quite feel whole without her. It's something our family is still dealing with." She took a deep breath and continued. "Two years ago I started a research project. I wanted to create a master list of the magical tomes that exist in the most well-known libraries, yours included.

"As I began to compile the list, I kept track of the most rare and dangerous of those books. Some of the books on the list are real, some based on old tales that haven't necessarily been proven to exist yet. Sometimes all I had was a mention in the margins of another book or a story about some legendary tome. My research hit snags here and there as I traced the books all around the globe throughout our history. Your records are quite helpful, by the way," she said as she looked up at Adelade, who blushed with pride.

"When the dark mage that Lee vanquished came to New Orleans, he was using a very old magic. As it turns out, he knew this magic because he was old himself—a former god who'd been cast out and made human as punishment.

"So six months ago, after the whole thing ended, I started looking into the base of his magic and found some really interesting stuff. My brother-in-law, Alex, has some relatives who are practicing the dark arts and as a result of some trial, their library was taken in a property settlement and awarded to Alex. He, in turn, gave me access to all of it."

"I'd heard. You must know, I was quite jealous, my dear. That collection is rumored to be one of the best libraries of dark magic tomes in recorded history. I've been trying to enlarge my own collection of dark magic texts but as you know, there's not a whole lot of goodwill that exists between practitioners on the path of light and dark magic users. If your brother-in-law ever decides to sell the collection you must contact me!" Adelade's face was lit up with the same kind of booklust that Em had and it endeared her to Em.

"Oh, Adelade, this collection is simply incredible. Some of it scared the hell out of me and I'm glad to say those books are now out of the reach of those who practice on the dark path. But so much knowledge, so much talent, the library simply hummed with it all." Em's face was dreamy.

"Anyway, if you can believe it, Alex's grandfather had a complete set of the *Necromancer's Journals*! I was researching through them and I kept coming across the same symbols in reference to an ancient tome or spell, something that I believe, if my translation is correct, is called *The Shifting Veil*, which supposedly contains a spellbook and ritual list for chaotic magic."

Em stopped speaking when the server brought their food. Once they'd eaten a bit she continued.

"Of course you see that chaotic magic of this type is the kind that can dissolve the Compact that we are bound by as well as other magical agreements and accords. I have reason to believe that the demon lord who attempted to break the Compact before is still looking for a way to do it. I must find this book."

Adelade had listened to Em intently. "And you think I have this book."

"Two things bring me your way, first—I traced some books from a collection that may have contained this book to an auction where you purchased at least part of it. According to the spotty records anyway. And second—yours is the most comprehensive collection of magical books in the world. It makes sense to come to you about this," Em said as she ate.

Adelade interrupted, "My collection is catalogued. If this book were in my collection it would be noted. You're welcome to come out and look, of course, but if I had it, I'm fairly sure I'd know."

"I know, and it's a great catalogue and I've been able to use part of your process with the Carter Collection. But I've looked and yes, it's not there by this name. But when I was looking into your collection I noticed that you have a rather large collection of dead language tomes and I'd like to check them over."

"Yes, I have a rather large collection of books that we just don't know what they are. They are in languages that no one can decipher. I suppose one of them could be the book you seek. The question being that if experts can't translate them, how can you?"

"I don't know for sure. I have some of the runic markings that accompanied the mention of this book. You know, of course, considering how old these books are that many of the volumes are handwritten. The markings I found in the *Journals* were written in the margins. I was hoping that I could match them somehow. I have a way with languages."

Adelade nodded. "A way? From what I understand, a gift is a better way to describe it. In any case, it sounds like a bloody time-consuming job. You are aware that there are probably at least a hundred books and manuscripts in that part of my library?"

Em nodded. "I figured as much. I'll try to stay out of your way and not bother you. I realize that I'm asking you to let me into your home and your collection and that would inconvenience you. I do appreciate it. I just can't give up and take the chance of this getting out and harming my family."

Adelade reached across the table and squeezed Em's hand. "It's no bother. I would be honored to have someone who loves books as much as you do in my library. A library isn't meant to be locked up, these books are meant to be seen and learned from. Come out whenever you wish, I'll alert my staff to make everything available to you should I be out when you call. In return, you have to allow me to visit to take a look through the Carter Collection."

Em smiled. "You've got a deal."

They spent the rest of the meal talking about the other books that Em had seen in her studies until Adelade looked up suddenly and smiled slyly. She stood.

"Well, dear, please come and see me soon. I'll be sure everything is ready. I look forward to talking with you again soon." Adelade gave her a kiss on her cheek and Em stood up to walk out with her when she turned to see Con standing there wearing that sexy smile.

"Mrs. Belton, shall I escort you to a cab?" Con asked, bowing over her hand and kissing it.

Adelade blushed and winked at Em. "Oh no, thank you, dear. I will get home my own way."

Em smiled, knowing that Adelade's "way" most likely would be magical and a cab was probably already waiting out there by calling spell or some such. Em waved and watched her leave after thanking her once more for her help.

Em looked back toward Con and blushed. "You really don't owe me anything, you know."

He pulled out her chair and helped her back into it, pulling his close with a hooked foot and sitting in it. "I know. I want to buy you a drink, Em. I want to know you."

For some reason, that shot straight to her gut. Things tightened low, moisture pooled and she had the strangest sense of already knowing Con MacNessa. She shook it off. "All right. I'll have a vodka tonic."

He gave her that smile again, the one that weakened her knees, and a server appeared instantly. She took their drink order and also brushed her breasts across Con's arm and shoulder several times until he'd had to physically turn himself from her and toward Em, who was glaring at the other woman.

"Does this happen a lot?" she asked, annoyed.

"What?" He couldn't take his eyes off her.

She waved her hand toward the women in the restaurant, who were all staring at him, and the bimbo waitress who'd rubbed her tits all over his arm. "When you're with one woman, you've got three more lining up to take her place." Suddenly she put her hand over her mouth, appalled.

He saw it and laughed, the sound tugged at her. She realized then how quiet it was. She usually had to deal with the rush of feelings from people, especially people who were in very close proximity, but she got nothing at all from Con. She couldn't read him at all. It felt peaceful but also slightly frightening, she rarely had to deal with other people without knowing their intentions. It was slightly puzzling though, there were only rare circumstances when she was unable to read other people—those people with certain levels of magical powers, like her sister, some people she was related to and a few people over her lifetime that she'd never quite known why.

"I hadn't noticed any other women, only you."

A shock of déjà vu hit her. He seemed so familiar—that moment, that phrase—as if she'd heard it before from his lips. She was very still and he homed in on it and moved so that his chair was touching hers.

"Em?" he purred.

"Y-yes?" she answered, his closeness making her clothes feel too tight. She warmed all over, skin tingling, nipples stabbing at the front of her sweater, begging for his attention. Cream flowed from her desire-softened pussy. She crossed her legs and squeezed her thighs together. The feeling was delicious. *So this is desire.*

Con reached out and traced the pad of a finger down the line of her cheek and along the fullness of her lips. A Cupid's bow bottom lip. His heart stuttered at how she felt beneath his finger. Satiny, sweet, full.

He leaned in to kiss her but the waitress all but slammed the drinks on the table. She leaned in between the two of them. "Anything else? Anything at all?" she breathed out.

Em snorted. "Oh god, could you be any more obvious? We get it, you want to sleep with him, but right now he's with me. If he's interested he'll let you know. Now, be on your way and don't think you'll be getting any tip."

The waitress looked at her, furious, and then back at Con, who shrugged and looked to Em again. She stomped off angrily.

Em blushed. She had no idea where her new assertiveness or her sense of possessiveness regarding Con was coming from but she liked them. She'd never felt possessive about a man before. Hell, except for the dream man, she'd never even felt desire before.

Em wanted to change her life, she wanted to do something different and take charge. She'd come all the way across the world to escape the shadow of her sister and the rest of her family and here she was, in a bar with an incredibly sexy man. She smiled at the thought that she just might let him talk her into sleeping with him.

"Thank you for defending my honor, Em," he said, grinning. He picked up her hand and kissed the tip of each one of her fingers, lightly biting each. He delighted in her shiver.

"What are you doing in London? Clearly you're an American. Southern perhaps?" he asked as he drew circles on the back of her hand with a thumb.

"Research," she said in a slightly broken voice. The stroke of his thumb on her hand was hypnotic. "Mrs. Belton has a private library. I'm here to do some research in it."

"What kind of research?"

Em felt the tickle up her spine and realized what he'd done. She might not be as powerful as Lee but she knew when someone was using magic on her. She snapped out of her erotic stupor and eyed him with hostility. "Back off!" she hissed and stood.

"What?" He cursed himself for attempting to use his magic to weave a truth spell on her. He tried to grab her arm but she pulled out of reach and headed toward the door. "Wait! Em, wait. What's wrong?" he called as she stormed outside.

She was tall and long-legged but he was, after all, taller and he caught up to her easily. He grabbed her arm and she tried to slap him with her free hand but he caught her easily and fended off the blow.

"Don't you think you owe me an explanation? One minute it looks like we're going to end up in bed and the next you're walking out on me!" The idea of her leaving made him feel panicky and he didn't like it. He'd never felt so vulnerable with a woman before.

"You're the most arrogant man! I owe you an explanation? Oh please! You tried a compulsion spell on me, you bastard. You're the one who owes an explanation, Con. Who are you? Is your name even Con? What's your game? Why are you trying to use magic on me?" she said, fury in her face.

And goddess if she weren't stunning at that moment. Her eyes flashing, lips parted, face flushed, hair in disarray. Even the way she stood was sexy, proud and erect, challenging him.

"Honestly, Em, there is no game. My name really is Con, or rather Conchobar. Con is what I've been called all of my life, like I'd guess you've been called Em for Emily your whole life." He paused. "As to the rest, please, let me explain. My hotel isn't far from here, we can go to my suite and speak privately."

"As if!" She laughed then and it flowed over him. *Well.* His sweet Em had the laugh of a siren, deep and velvety. Combining that with her anger found him even more deeply enmeshed in her spell.

"I promise that nothing will happen that you don't want to happen. What we need to talk about isn't for public consumption and you know it. The Belleville is a reputable hotel, you'll be safe."

"You're staying at the Belleville?" She eyed him narrowly.

"Yes, I just said so, didn't I? We can go to your hotel if you wish."

She couldn't explain it but she trusted him not to harm her and she didn't want to leave his presence just then. Clearly he had some kind of magic. She couldn't read him and the spell he used was subtle, more subtle than any she'd ever experienced. If she hadn't been so hyperaware of him at that moment, she probably wouldn't have felt it at all. He was right, they couldn't talk about it in public and she didn't have the ability to do a privacy spell like the one Adelade had conjured.

"All right. But my brother-in-law owns the Belleville and I'll have you removed and call the cops if you try anything funny, buster."

He let out the breath he'd been holding and then it hit him. "Aidan Bell is your brother-in-law?"

"You know Aidan?"

"Yes, I haven't seen him in…a while, but yes, we're acquainted. Come, let's go, it's obvious we have a lot to talk about."

She eyed him narrowly and fell into step beside him.

At the Belleville they all rushed to help her and Con wanted to slap them all away. She was his woman and watching the way the bellman touched her arm as he opened the door for her made Con sick with jealousy.

She smiled at the concierge and informed him that she would be in Mr. MacNessa's room and to ring her there if any calls came in for her. Con wanted to laugh, none of these mortals could stop him should he desire to harm her, he could transport them to any spot in this world or his own in the blink of an eye. But it made her feel safe and so he merely smiled and held the elevator for her.

* * * * *

Em sat on the couch in the sitting area of the suite, watching Con as he moved about the room.

"Can I get you something from the bar? A sparkling water? A beer? Another vodka tonic?" he asked her casually.

"You can get to the point. What are you and why did you use a compulsion spell on me?" She would have been appalled by her lack of manners if she hadn't been so angry with him.

He sat on the low table in front of the couch. "I'm merely curious about your research. I could sense you were a witch, I just wanted to know what you were up to. Nothing nefarious, just basic nosiness."

"How could you sense that? What are you that you not only have your own magic but you could sense mine?"

He spun the possible responses through his mind. "I'm a wizard," he said at last.

"Is that so? What family are you from?"

Damn! He'd underestimated her. "The MacNessa family. We're Irish."

She rolled her eyes and made that incorrect game show buzzer sound. "Wrong. No such family. I've just completed an exhaustive wizarding family tree, the fruit of a year of research and a brother-in-law who belongs to one of the most powerful wizarding families in the world. Try again." She crossed her arms over her chest, distracting him further as the action thrust her breasts up higher.

Before he could say anything else his phone rang and he picked it up, relieved to be given a momentary reprieve.

The call was for Em and he handed the phone over.

"Hello?"

"Em? Are you all right? I've been trying to call you on your cell phone but you weren't answering and you weren't in your room. I've been frantic!" her sister babbled out in a jumbled rush of words.

"Whoa! What's going on? Is everything all right?"

"Why didn't you answer your phone, why aren't you in the penthouse, just who is this man?" Lee demanded.

"I left my phone here at the hotel. I was at dinner and I had an interesting conversation that I came back here to continue in private. Why are you calling, Lee?" Em was over her worry and had now moved to annoyed that her sister would call her across the world simply to lecture her.

"I had a waking dream. I saw you, you were sitting and you met an older woman and then you bumped into a man on the street. He struck a chord in you. I woke up and I've been trying to call you ever since!"

"Ah. Well, that's pretty much what has happened. In fact, put Aidan on, will you?"

"What? NO! Tell me what the hell is going on! You can't just not tell me, for god's sake. You're in some guy's room and you're in a foreign country. First, hello is he cute? And second, I know he's not an ax murderer or you'd have felt it, but he's still a stranger. What does he want from you?"

She sighed. She knew Lee was just concerned about her and she softened her tone. "Listen, I'm trying to figure that out myself. I promise to tell you everything once I work it out. Now please just put Aidan on."

Con was eyeing her suspiciously.

"Hello, darlin', is something wrong with the hotel? Can I help?" Aidan asked as he came on the line.

"No, it's wonderful here, thank you for letting me use the penthouse, it's amazing. I have a question. Do you know a Conchobar MacNessa?"

"Con? You know him? Where is he?" Aidan demanded.

"He's right here, he's been dodging my questions. He tried to use magic on me and I caught him. At this moment he looks like he swallowed his tongue because he told me he knew you and now you're going to tell me what the hell is going on."

Aidan smiled despite himself. He'd never heard Em like this and he liked it. "Con is a Faerie, a very old one. He's favored by their queen. He's tricky, but generally trustworthy. A revered and fearsome warrior. But, Em, he likes women, *a lot*. Be careful of him."

Em eyed Con and he knew instantly that she'd just found out he was Fae.

"Thank you for telling me, Aidan. Please inform my sister of what was said so I don't have to repeat it."

Aidan laughed, Lee had been dancing around him, trying to hear what was going on. He knew she'd be drilling him for information once he hung up. "Put Con on for a moment please, sweet."

She handed the phone to Con who took it suspiciously. "Aidan, how are you?"

"I'm good, never better in fact. I've got a wife, I'm living in New Orleans and I've got a really special sister-in-law. Con, if you fuck her over I'll hunt you down," Aidan said, his voice going low and dangerous.

"I respect that. It won't be necessary, Aidan. I want the opposite—like I've never wanted anything before." And it scared the pants off him.

"She's the one?"

"Capital T, capital O. Ten thousand years have passed and nothing prepared me for this."

Aidan began to laugh. "Is that so? Have you told Em this yet?"

"No. I just met her a few hours ago. It's a bit much at this stage."

"Have you dealt with human women before, Con? They are, uh, less than malleable, not like vampire females, that's for sure. I found that out," he said the last quietly, not wanting to raise Lee's ire. "You can't just keep her in the dark, she won't appreciate it."

"I know, I'll explain when it's time," Con assured him.

"And why were you using a compulsion spell on her? You'd better not be trying to force your way with her." Menace crept back into his tone.

Con was insulted. He'd never, not once in ten thousand years, taken a woman with magic or by force. "You should know better than that, Aidan. As for why I did it, it's complicated but trust me, it wasn't to hurt her."

"Remember what I said. Hurt her and I drink every ounce of that ten-thousand-year-old blood in your veins," Aidan warned.

Con reassured him again of his intentions, and unable to postpone the inevitable, Aidan said goodbye and hung up.

Em watched him with one elegantly arched brow raised. "So, let's go back to the beginning, shall we? Who and what are you and why did you use magic on me?"

He sat next to her on the couch, as close as he could without causing her to move away from him. "I really am Con MacNessa and I really am curious about your research. I'm also a Faerie, that's where my magic comes from."

"I've never met a Faerie. For some reason, I'd always imagined them to be small and have wings."

He scowled, obviously she'd hit a sore point and she struggled not to laugh. "Do I look small to you?"

"I don't know, I haven't seen all of you," she teased and then gasped at herself. "God, an hour with you and I'm suddenly not in control of my tongue."

"Well, I know how we can combine you seeing just how big I am and some tongue control," he leaned in and said in a sexy growl. Her eyes slid halfway closed and she moaned softly.

She put her hand, palm flat, against his chest and pushed him back. "You haven't answered the question. If you were just curious, why not ask more pointed questions? It seems a bit of overkill to use a compulsion spell for ordinary inquisitiveness. Thing is, Con, given the smooth way you've been talking me up tonight and the way you seized the moment when you bumped into me, I don't take you for a very overkill kind of man. No, you seem to be all about subtlety."

"Look, why don't you tell me about your research and I can tell you more after that?" he suggested.

She backed up from him and he watched her shields come up. "Why are you so interested?"

He saw something in her eyes, fear? He reached out to touch her but she stood up and moved away. His heart felt squeezed by that, by her holding herself away from him. "Are you afraid of me? Em, I may not be being totally honest with you right now, but you never have reason to fear me. I would never hurt you."

She heard the hurt in his voice and nearly relented until she remembered that a demon lord wanted to destroy her family. For all she knew this Faerie was working with the bad guys. Why else would a total stranger be so interested in her work? It was clear he had some idea of what she was doing, but how could he? She hadn't told anyone other than Adelade earlier that evening and that happened after he bumped into her. A sickening realization that had been tickling the back of her mind came to her then.

"Your bumping into me tonight wasn't an accident." It wasn't a question. She knew the answer. "You set me up."

"No. I mean, no it wasn't an accident, but I didn't set you up. I wanted to meet you to talk with you about your research."

Her heart fell then. Whatever he was after, it wasn't her. She felt like a fool for believing that a man who looked like Con would be interested in her. She started toward the door. "Fuck you, Con MacNessa," she said as she grabbed the knob.

He was behind her, his hands flat on the door, holding it closed, body caging her in. "What do you think you're doing? You can't just walk out."

"I can and I will. I'm not interested in what you're selling. Now get the hell out of my way. I'll let you stay here tonight but I'm calling Aidan to have him boot your ass out tomorrow morning." She kept facing the door, the heat radiating off his body was making her dizzy.

He placed his lips at her ear and ground his cock into her ass. "Oh I do think you want it, I can smell how wet you are."

She closed her eyes against the potency of his words, of his presence. "I want you to move out of my way or I'll scream," she ground out, face red with humiliation. He knew his game had worked on her and now he was taunting her.

He sighed and took a step back. She pulled the door open and stalked out without looking back at him.

* * * * *

Em slammed back into the penthouse and ran herself a very hot bath in the giant bathtub. The nerve of that jerk to use her that way! She tossed her clothes in a heap and slowly stepped into the steaming water, sinking with a sigh of satisfaction.

To think she'd actually liked the way she had been unable to read him. She'd felt confident of her allure as a woman, that she didn't need the failsafe of her gift with this man. Now she felt like a fool.

For a short time that night she'd felt desire, had felt desired, but it was all a lie to manipulate her. Lee probably wouldn't have been taken in by such flamboyant tactics, although he probably wouldn't have had to fake it with Lee.

The tears came then until her body was racked with sobs.

Downstairs in his suite, Con couldn't stand it another second. He had to make her talk to him. Sure, he'd arranged to meet her but that didn't mean she had to get all huffy about it.

He shimmered into the penthouse and the sound of her sobs slammed into him, staggering him.

He ran toward her, wanting to stop the terrible pain he was hearing. He wanted to kill whoever made her cry like that. He burst into the bathroom and she jumped up with her hands out in defense, a look of fear on her face.

A face that was swollen with tears. He also couldn't help but notice that she looked like a water nymph standing there, beads of water gliding down her long, lean thighs, her breasts high and full, capped with raspberry pink nipples. She was glistening and lithe, her eyelashes wet with tears, steam rising about her as she stood, fragile and defensive.

"Em! Are you all right, *a ghra?*" he asked, walking to her.

She backed up, covering her nakedness with her arms. "W-what are you doing here? Get out!"

"Who made you cry? Tell me and I'll kill him immediately," he ordered imperiously.

She looked at him incredulously. "What? Get out!"

Ignoring her orders, he kept walking toward her, thought his clothes away and stepped into the bath with her.

"Meep!" she exclaimed incoherently as she tried, and failed, not to look at his naked body. For a jerk he had a glorious body, hard and muscled, that golden skin stretched taut over it. Yep, nothing small there, she thought to herself as she tore her eyes away from their perusal of his cock.

"Do you like what you see, *a thaisce?*" he murmured as he stood before her.

Em had to close her eyes. His voice was temptation. She ached to believe his attraction was real and when she snuck another quick peek south, his cock certainly seemed interested. Outside of her dreams and magazines, she'd never seen a naked man and this one was certainly a fine first.

"What are you calling me? What language is that?" she managed to get out as she pressed herself back against the wall, getting as far from him as she could and still be in the tub.

"It's Gaelic. I'll tell you later what it means. For now, why don't you tell me why you're so upset so I may kill whoever made you this way?"

She rolled her eyes at him. "You're going to kill yourself?"

"I made you cry?" He looked stunned. He stepped up to her until they were touching and pulled her to him, his hands at her waist, his face against her bare shoulder. She pushed at him but he held fast. "I am sorry, the last thing I wish to do is bring you sorrow."

She stopped struggling. She could hear the tenderness in his words, feel it as he held her body. He was pushing past her resolve and she had no way to stop him. "I can't tell if you're for real," she whispered.

He moved, deliberately sliding his body along hers. Even though Em was only two inches shy of six feet, he still towered above her, easily standing at over six and a half feet. "How can you not know I am real? Can you not feel the pounding of my heart?" He took her hand and placed it palm flat on his chest. "Can you not see it in my eyes? Hear it in my voice? Feel my desire for you here?" He ground his hard cock against her belly.

"I've been able to read people my entire life. I can always trust my power because it doesn't lie. I can't read you, Con, and it scares me. I know you've lied to me. By rights I should be screaming my head off and kicking you out of here but I'm standing, naked, with you in the bathtub. You make me do things I wouldn't normally do."

He sighed and his breath felt cool against her heated flesh. He smelled like sandalwood and fresh air. "*A ghra*, I cannot tell you the whole truth right now. I can't. I'm sorry but I will tell you when I can, I promise. One thing that is absolutely true is that I would never hurt you. I want you. You don't need special powers to feel what's between us, do you?"

How the heck would she know about what was between them? Sure it felt different than she'd ever felt about a man before, but she was a freaking virgin! It's not like she'd ever let a naked man into her bathtub before, much less a ten-thousand-year-old warrior Faerie.

At that, a giggle bubbled up and he looked down at her with surprise. "Sorry. I thought of something funny. And, uh, what I can feel between us, well, sure it's real, unless it's a glamour. You Faeries can do that right? The glamour thing?"

He threw back his head and laughed. "Oh, *mo fiach*! I can do a glamour but I can't fake a hard cock—you made it that way just by existing. I've had this," he lowered his chin in the direction of his cock, "ever since the first moment I saw you."

"Enough with the sneaky use of foreign words! What are you calling me?"

He chuckled and kissed her nose. He pulled her down into the water and between the cradle of his thighs. "*Mo fiach* means my raven. Your hair, it's as dark as a raven's wing."

"My *grandmere* calls me little raven, even though I'm nearly a foot taller than she is. That's what they called me when I was a baby."

Con began to soap up her shoulders. "You see, I know you. You can feel that in your heart, can't you?"

"I can't believe I'm sitting naked in my bathtub with a total stranger," she muttered.

"Ah, but we established that I'm not a stranger, didn't we? I know you. Look within yourself, you know me."

She turned around to face him. "And what of the glamour? You said you couldn't fake that," she pointed at his lap, "but you didn't say if you were using a glamour in any other way. I mean, you are ten thousand years old. Are you withered and gray and hunchbacked with no teeth?"

He sat silently, thinking. Making up his mind, he stood up and pulled her with him. "Let me dry you and I'll tell you," he said and helped her out of the tub. He dried her with a big, soft towel, rubbing her skin in small, sensual circles.

She was oh-so-wet thinking about him. Her nipples were hard and she'd given up blaming it on the room being cold. She wanted him inside her, over her. A trickle of honey oozed from her pussy. Seeing it, Con growled and leaned in, lapping it up in a long swipe of his tongue.

"Oh my god," Em said, voice trembling.

"You taste so good, I've never tasted anything so tempting," he murmured, his brown eyes looking up into hers.

He stood up and led her into the bedroom. "I mean to have you, *mo fiach*. Again and again." He sat her down on the bed. "But first, are you ready to see me without the glamour?"

She nodded, mute.

While she was staring at him, it was as if he blurred for a moment and then got solid again and she jumped back with a gasp, pushing her back against the headboard shaking her head. "No! It can't be…"

He stood there with golden eyes and long caramel hair, braids at his temples. He was even taller than before and, *oh my*, his cock was longer and thicker. The rest of his body was the same, hard and muscled.

Her heart pounded at the realization. That exact moment was part of a dream she'd had over and over. How many times had she woken up aching and wet after looking up at this naked warrior looking down at her, cock hard and ready, watching her like a rapacious predator? She'd lost count. She just hoped he did eat her up in three bites.

"It can't be what? You're making me nervous. Do I not please you?" he asked, irritated and nervous.

"Have you looked in a mirror lately? What woman wouldn't be pleased by a naked you standing at the foot of their bed?" she said agitatedly. She had no idea how to tell him she'd been dreaming of him — of that exact moment — since she was fourteen years old.

The sly smile came back and he relaxed. He reached out and grabbed her ankle and dragged her across the bed toward him.

"I'm going to fuck you until you can't move. But first I'm going to eat your pussy until you scream my name."

She shivered and closed her eyes against him. She had no defenses where he was concerned. Her logical mind knew how stupid it was to have sex with a stranger, especially one who'd lied to her, but her body didn't care. Her heart didn't care. This was her dream man, the man she'd had in her head and who'd occupied and owned her heart for so long.

He leaned over her and stroked his hair across her skin, across her pebbled nipples, down over her belly and across her mound, swirling it around her knees and toes. It felt like the touch of velvet over her flushed skin. She let out a shaky breath.

"Open your eyes, Em. I want you to see who is bringing you pleasure," he ordered.

She dragged her eyes open and looked at him, watched as he moved up toward her, crawling over her body and taking her lips with his own. He coaxed her at first, bringing her out of her shell until she'd opened her mouth under his and his tongue flicked into her mouth, over her gums and the inside her cheeks. He tasted of mint and wine, she couldn't get enough and writhed to get closer to him. He answered her silent plea and let his body rest completely on hers, his weight at once overwhelming and anchoring.

She smoothed her hands up his biceps and shoulders, over the planes of his muscles. His skin was hot and she absorbed his heat into her hands. His hair was a curtain around them, walling them in and making her feel as if there was no one in the universe but the two of them.

She sucked on his tongue and he gave a ragged cry. Her hands were now fisted in his hair, the silk of it caressing the flesh of her arms. He kissed the line of her jaw, his tongue flicking out, tasting her.

She drove him wild. The way her body felt beneath his own, the feel of her nipples against his chest, the soapy clean smell of her skin and the subtle citrus scent of her shampoo. Her hands held his head to her as if she were making an offering. Each taste of her drove him up higher, testing his restraint. He wanted to take it slow, make it an incremental slide into her pleasure, so that her time with him would wipe any other man from her mind. But with each small sigh, each brush of her very wet pussy against his thigh or his belly it battered at him, pushing him closer to the point where all he'd have left would be to shove himself inside her and ride her until they both were boneless.

His lips skimmed along the graceful column of her neck and he laved the hollow of her throat, feasting on her fluttering pulse. He nibbled across her collarbone and slowly down the curve of her breast until she cried out when he slowly sucked her turgid nipple into his mouth, grazing it with his teeth.

"Oh!" she exclaimed with wonder. One hand rolled and tugged on a nipple while his mouth scorched the other. He alternately swirled his tongue around the peak and then bit it, laving the sting and pulling it, hard, to the roof of his mouth. "Don't stop, oh god, that feels so good," she whispered, barely holding onto herself. She felt as if she was falling and she didn't know how to stop, how to get a grip. There was simply no way she could have ever imagined pleasure like this. She'd given herself pleasure before but it was nothing compared to the feelings that Con evoked with his mouth and hands.

He looked up at her, his lips slightly swollen, eyes wicked and golden. "You're so responsive, I'll bet I can make you come just by sucking your nipples."

She nodded, biting her bottom lip and tasting blood, she was so close to begging him to do just that.

He buried his face between her breasts and laved a tongue down her breastbone, his fingers softly tracing down each rib and feathering over her hipbones. She gasped and arched into him when he tongued her navel. His hair dragging down her body felt like another set of hands stroking her flesh. She was panting now, waiting to feel what he'd do next.

But nothing in her life until that moment could have prepared her for the way it felt when he pushed her thighs apart and up, opening her to his gaze. He blew across her swollen, glistening flesh and she cried out. She tried to close her thighs against him — it was too much. Her face burned with embarrassment.

"Don't fight against it. You're so beautiful here, pink and pearly with your juice. I've already tasted you, I want more and you're going to give it to me, Em," he said as he touched her clit with the tip of his tongue, just a quick flick.

She shuddered, right on the verge of coming. He felt her clit pulse beneath his tongue, it swelled up further and she gushed cream. He groaned at the sight, at the scent and feel of her raining honey for him.

He backed away from her clit and tongued her, making big, round, wet circles through the folds of her flesh, nibbling on her labia while she trembled. Her hands tightened in his hair and his control slipped another notch. He stabbed his tongue into her core and she let out a guttural groan and arched into him, pressing her pussy against his face. He held her up higher, his hands under her ass, holding her to him like a piece of ripe, juicy fruit. He watched her cream flow down and over her pretty pink rosette and lapped it up there, eliciting a shocked gasp from her. He knew he'd be back later for that hole and that he'd be the first to breach it. It gave him a savage thrill of possession.

He stroked a finger into her and his cock nearly exploded when he felt how tight she was. The walls of her pussy were silky and molten and she gripped his finger and arched, riding him when he added another to stretch her. He knew that he wouldn't last very long once he got inside her, even if he recited the entire history of the Tuatha De Danann in his head.

"You're so tight, the way you're gripping my fingers is making me crazy," he said in a low voice.

She had no voice to tell him she was a virgin. He'd taken her to a place where all she could do was feel, take in the sensations he was creating. It was all she could do to process them without screaming. She whimpered when he found her clit again with his tongue and he chuckled, the vibrations pulsing through her. When he sucked it into his mouth, teeth grazing across the hood and tongue lapping the underside, time stopped for a moment, and then everything exploded into white-hot feeling. She cried out his name and her back bowed off the mattress. He kept his face pressed into her, relentlessly pushing her higher and higher, holding her to him by her hips. He continued to suck her clit and fuck her with his fingers until she came again, a second climax that pulled a scream from her, her head thrashing from side to side.

He pulled away from her and she watched through passion-stunned eyes as he licked his lips and took his cock in his hand. "I need to fuck you, Em. I need to be inside of you right now." He knelt between her thighs and put them over his own, putting a pillow under her bottom.

"Yes, please fuck me, Con. I need you." She felt achy inside, empty, and she wanted him to fill her up. When she felt the fat, broad head brush up against her gate she blinked her eyes, trying to surface. "Wait, condom…"

"Don't need one. No human STDs and I can't get you pregnant unless I want to," he said and plunged into her, realizing too late that she'd never been fucked before.

Her face, just glazed over with desire, was now pinched in pain.

"Why didn't you tell me!" He concentrated on not coming, on not moving. He didn't want to hurt her any more, wanted to let her adjust to his size.

She reached up and touched his face, her thumb tracing over his bottom lip. "It doesn't matter. It was always meant to be you," she whispered with a smile.

The tenderness in her face squeezed his heart. He'd bedded a lot of women in his lifetime, thousands of them, and never, not once, did a single one of them make him feel so powerful, so trusted and invincible. She filled every part of him at that moment. Her soul mingled with his own and he felt like he was capable of anything simply because she looked at him the way she did.

"It'll get better, just try and relax." He reached between them and found her clit and slowly stroked over it. He felt her loosen up as he slowly stoked her fire, she grew slicker, creamier and he moved slowly, pulling himself out and then pushing back in. She gave a sigh then, a sound of pleasure, and he leaned down and nipped her bottom lip. "You're so damned sexy I don't think I'll be able to let you out of this bed for days."

She laughed and it sounded like birds flying free, the sound soared in the air. The tightness that she'd had in her chest for the last year loosened. She felt as if she were truly free and utterly herself for the first time in her life.

Her laugh turned into a groan of pleasure as he pushed back inside her. "Put your legs around my waist," he said with a grunt and when she did, it opened her even more. Her breasts swayed with movement, her skin glistened with sweat as he moved within her. She wore a look of joyous discovery on her face as she looked into his eyes. Her hands stroked over his nipples and she delighted in his moan. She slid them down his sides and grabbed the rock-hard cheeks of his perfect ass, pulling him deeper inside her deeper.

He changed his angle and she gasped at the feel of his cock head brushing over her in a new way. The place he was rubbing against created pleasure so sharp it was almost too much. He grinned at her wickedly and plumped her clit between thumb and forefinger just as he brushed the spot of nerves inside her. She screamed out her climax, her pussy clamping down on him like a vise. The wave of pleasure drowned her. She clawed at his back, meeting his thrusts in an almost frenzied manner.

"Oh that's so fucking good," he grunted. "Your pussy is squeezing me so tight I think I may die from it." His speed picked up as he fucked her hard and deep, her body sucking him back inside, her juices flowing, slick and welcoming. His head flew back and he came with a hoarse roar as he bathed her with jet after jet of his cum.

Ripples of intense pleasure rolled through him as his orgasm went on and on, back arched, cock touching her womb, her legs clutching his waist, her nails digging into the flesh of his shoulders, pussy grasping and fluttering around him. Finally, what seemed like an hour later, he let out a long gasp and collapsed next to her, pulling her into the shelter of his body.

Her muscles were twitching, her pulse hammering. Her body felt deliciously battered. She snuggled back into him and sighed.

Chapter Three

ஐ

They both must have slept for some time because it was beginning to get light when she opened her eyes to find him looking down at her with such longing that it made her stomach clench. She smiled. "Hi."

He leaned down and kissed her softly. "You should have told me you were a virgin, Em. Are you all right? I know I hurt you. I'm sorry."

She laughed and sat up. "I'm not hurt. It's sweet of you to worry but really, I'm all right. Better than all right, I'm fantastic. Thank you. They say you never forget your first time but those poor suckers sure don't get a man like you to remember." She stretched and couldn't hide her wince as she stood up.

"I'm going to run you a bath," he said. "The soreness will ease in the hot water."

"I'm guessing that there'll be some healing herbs in the bathroom. You won't find any place a Charvez spends any amount of time in without them and this is my sister's apartment. They'll help." She started to walk into the bathroom but he swung her up into his arms.

"Tell me where they are, I'll get them." His voice was tight and his mouth was in a flat line. His forehead was creased into a big, angry frown.

She looked inside the cabinet and found the jar, dark glass to keep the herbs fresh and potent, and he poured them into the tub as the water ran.

He helped her inside and sank down next to the tub.

"Aren't you coming in with me?" she asked.

"No," he said tersely.

Her heart fell. "You don't have to stay if you don't want to. I won't make a scene or anything," she said with a coolness she didn't feel.

He grabbed her chin and turned her face to his. "You can't brush me off so easily. I'm here to stay, you'd better get used to it."

"Why are you so angry with me? I'm sorry I wasn't some super sex goddess, I'm sure you've been with women who are better and more experienced at sex than I am." Her voice trembled and her bottom lip was threatening to actually pout. She was mortified but she couldn't help it.

He stroked over her with a soft washcloth and looked up, surprised. He saw her upset face and he gentled. "What the hell are you talking about? I'm angry because you didn't tell me you were a virgin and I hurt you. If I'd have known I would have entered you more slowly instead of plunging inside."

Feeling mollified, she leaned back against the edge of the tub and closed her eyes as he ran the cloth over her skin in large, soapy circles. "I liked you plunging inside. Okay, so it hurt more than I thought it would at first, but after I got used to it, it felt really, really good." She opened her eyes and looked at him. "In fact, when can we do it again? I'd like to return the favor and go down on you. I probably won't be very good at it in the beginning but I'm a very fast learner."

Against his better judgment, he laughed at her earnestness. Leaning in, he kissed her shoulder. "We should wait, you're sore."

She dunked under the water and stood up, the water sluicing down her body. "No, I'm not, but you can make me that way. Some aches are better if they're well-earned."

"What have I created?" he murmured.

She quirked up a corner of her mouth and held out her hand to him. "And anyway, my mouth isn't sore at all and I've always wanted to know what a cock tastes like."

The body part in question swelled up in response. "Wait." He tugged on her hand. "Let me take a quick shower and I'll be right out."

"I can help you," she said in a sexy murmur.

"I know, but I'd end up fucking you standing up against the tiles and I want your lips around my cock first. Wait for me in the bedroom. I'll be in in a few minutes."

"Oh, all right. Spoilsport. Do Faeries drink wine? There's a great bottle of cabernet open."

"Yes, we drink wine and I'd love a glass."

She smiled at him and sauntered out and he nearly put an eye out as he walked into the glass enclosure around the shower.

* * * * *

When he walked into the bedroom ten minutes later she was laying naked on the chaise near the French doors leading to the terrace. The morning sun was lighting her creamy skin, she looked magical, sultry and sexy.

She stood and walked toward him, holding out a glass of wine. "It's early for alcohol, it feels so hedonistic to be standing naked before a drop-dead sexy man with a glass of wine in my hand at seven in the morning. I like it."

"As long as I'm the only man you're standing naked in front of, that's fine with me. We can do this every morning as far as I'm concerned." He drank the wine and placed the glass down on the table. He took her glass from her hands and put it next to his.

Tossing a pillow on the floor, he grabbed her, his large hand gentle around her neck, and pulled her close. With lips barely touching hers he growled, "Now on your knees and suck my cock."

She shuddered as the dark command made her pussy weep. She slowly slid to her knees before him. "Tell me what to do, what you like," she whispered, looking up at him.

His hands cradled her skull and his thumbs traced over her eyebrows tenderly. "Take me into your mouth, just the head."

He jerked at the sensation of her hot, wet mouth sliding over his cock head.

"Touch my balls, yes, like that," he said. She held him in the palm of her hand and rolled them gently. The other hand was holding him at the root of his cock, keeping him steady as her mouth was on him. "Hold me tighter."

She gripped him tighter and he hissed when she dipped her tongue into his weeping slit. She swirled her tongue around him. "That's it, baby. Right there, underneath the head, oh yeah," he mumbled as she found the sensitive spot and flicked her tongue over it. "Use your teeth."

She lightly scraped her teeth over the sweet spot and dragged her fingernails gently over his balls. She could feel the veins beneath her hand pulsing as he grew harder. His balls drew tight against his body.

"That's sooo good." He took her hand and pulled the skin down, tightening it. She took more of him into her mouth, keeping the skin of his cock taut.

She gloried in the feel of him. She'd always thought of blowjobs with slight unease but this was incredible. Just feeling the changes of his body as her mouth was on him, how much each little thing she did affected him, turned him on... It turned her on. Her pussy was clenching, reaching for him to fill her up. He tasted salty and tangy and his skin was silky but he was oh-so-hard.

He stroked gently into her mouth, careful not to go too deep. He was too big for her to take all of him. It was difficult to believe this was her first time, she was turning him on more than he'd ever been before. Her mouth over his flesh was paradise. He looked down at her and watched his cock disappear into her mouth and come out again, wet with saliva, glistening and red, Her hair, dark as night, contrasted against the Sidhe gold of his skin.

"Oh fuck, you're so good. I'm going to come," he managed to get out, turned on beyond bearing as he thought about being the first man to shoot his seed down that pretty throat. That thought pushed him over and he came with a roar, his hands tightening in her hair, holding her to him as burst after burst of hot cum hit the back of her throat.

She swallowed over and over and licked him clean as she pulled her mouth from him. He slumped onto the chaise and she moved to sit on the pillow, her cheek on his thigh. He said nothing for a while as his hands stroked through her hair.

After a bit she turned and knelt between his thighs. "I really liked that. How'd I do?"

Her enthusiasm was touching and very sexy. "You did great, and I really liked it too," he said with a chuckle. He moved so that his back was against the arm of the chaise and his legs stretched out in front of him. "You there with the light behind you like that, it's one of the most beautiful things I've ever seen. Come here, straddle my thighs."

She licked her lips and obeyed. He positioned her so that her pussy was over his reviving cock. "You're scalding hot," he murmured and pulled her down, rubbing her over him, bathing his cock in her juices.

Her eyes glazed over. "Yes," she hissed.

He grabbed her hips, stroking her over his cock slowly, grinding against her. "Move so that I can suck your nipples," he ordered after she'd gotten the rhythm down. She whimpered and moved her upper body forward. "Hold your breasts up for me."

She cupped her breasts and offered them up to his eager mouth. She sighed at the incredible feeling each time his mouth tugged on her nipple. The shock of pleasure jolted her as she rubbed her pussy over his cock. She went up on her knees, raising herself so that she could put him inside her but he shook his head. "No, you're sore and it's too soon. I want you to come this way, bathe my cock with that cream gushing out of you."

Her movements became less controlled as he ramped her up. He slid a hand behind her, down the crack of her ass, dipping his fingers into her wetness and then back up to tickle over the pucker of her rear passage. He slowly pushed a finger inside as he began to focus her weight over the head of his cock, letting it brush her clit over and over. This in concert with his finger slowly thrusting into her tight rear passage. He watched the flush work its way up her skin, her nipples getting darker, harder, elongating. He sucked one hard nipple into his mouth and bit down and she threw her head back and came on a silent scream as she ground herself desperately onto him, her anus clamping down on his finger. His cock, knowing when it had a good thing, shot until the two of them were reduced to a warm, wet heap of twitching muscles.

Chapter Four

☞

The next time she woke up it was due to hunger. She looked at the bedside clock and discovered that it was after eleven. The sun sat high in the sky and she sat up, feeling muscles she'd forgotten existed but wearing a satisfied smile. Boy, she might have been a late bloomer in the sex department but once she got started she really did it right.

Speaking of that, she looked around. Con was nowhere to be found. She shrugged and called out his name but he didn't answer. She got up and ran yet another bath with the healing herbs. She sank into the water and picked up the phone to check her messages.

With a sigh she listened to them all. As she'd predicted, her family had decided that she was a total infant and unable to be away without constant supervision. There were messages from both of her brothers. Eric sounded amused but Niall sounded perturbed that she hadn't been there to answer her phone. Her father had called once, reminding her that in London they call the police bobbies and that she should call the hotel if there was an emergency because Aidan had set it up for them to help her should she need it.

She rolled her eyes as she went through the three from Lee ordering her to call and explain what was happening. She knew she'd have to call her mother back—one didn't ignore *Maman*'s messages—but she'd call the others back later, on her own schedule.

She loved her family for their concern but resented it at the same time. That they thought she was so ill-prepared to deal with the basics of life just showed how little they understood her. And how could that be? Em knew that being the youngest child made the others see her as a responsibility. They all felt protective of her. She knew that they understood the strain of constantly being bombarded with the emotions of everyone around her and that they had sought to keep things calm for her when she was younger just to save her nerves. But she wasn't eight years old she was twenty-five!

Quickly calculating the time difference, she dialed the phone number. They should be awake. Regardless, her mother had said to call back no matter what time it was and so she did.

"Hello?" Her mother's richly accented voice came over the line and Em smiled, even through her annoyance.

"*Maman*, how are you?"

"*Cher*, I'm good but not as good as you, eh?" her mother said with a laugh.

"What?"

"Something happened to you last night, yes? Something important. I felt it. Just as I felt when your sister was with Aidan that first time. Your heart has found her partner."

"Oh, I don't know that I'd go that far. I also don't know if I should be creeped out that my mother knows I had sex."

Her mother laughed. "*Cher*, I know you've waited twenty-five years to do it and it must have meant a lot for you to do it now. I hope this man understands the gift you've given him. Is this Faerie worthy of your love, Em?"

"Whoa! Love is jumping the gun a bit, *Maman*. And how did you know he was a Faerie?" She gritted her teeth—damn that Lee! "Anyway, sure I like him—a lot—but I don't know him well enough to be in love with him."

"Who are you trying to convince, sug? Charvez women don't dally. We love. You especially. You've turned your nose up at every interested male for the last twenty-five years. You don't take sex lightly. You wouldn't have shared yourself with him if you didn't love him."

"I'm not in London to get a boyfriend. I have work to do. Con is fun and sexy and smart but he's also quite the ladies' man according to Aidan, who I'm sure you've talked to or you wouldn't have known Con was a Faerie."

Her mother made an indistinct Gallic sound and Em could see the accompanying elegant shrug in her mind's eye. "Eh, so? Your father was notorious with women when I met him. From that moment on he was only notorious with me. Your grandfather was the same. Aidan and Alex too."

She blocked out the image of her father as a ladies' man and laughed. "Thanks for the visuals, *Maman*. I'm sure that's burned into my brain forever. I have to go. I've slept the morning away and the bathwater is getting cold."

"Em, you be careful. I know you are there for an important reason, more than just to look at a library. I can feel that it could be dangerous if you don't pay attention. Dark forces are always watching and waiting for a way to succeed. You might try to share what you're up to with your family."

Leave it to her mother to get all witchy. "I'll be careful. I'll be able to explain more when I get home. I love you."

"And I you," her mother said with a sigh, letting the issue go — for the moment, anyway.

Smiling, Em got out of the tub and dried off. She dressed in a pair of jeans and a light blouse. She discovered that breakfast had been delivered while she'd been sleeping and poured a cup of coffee from the carafe that kept it hot. She ate the fruit and cheese and crusty bread. A distinctly French breakfast for a London hotel. Then again, Aidan probably told them what she liked.

She wondered where Con had gone. She tried not to think that he'd thought of last night as a one-night stand. She sure hoped it was more because her mother, as usual, was right. She was more than halfway in love with Conchobar MacNessa, the man of her dreams.

Pushing that to the back of her mind, she grabbed her bag and headed out. A car was waiting to take her to Oxford to meet with an old friend who was a scholar specializing in magical languages. She hoped that he might be able to help her decipher the symbols from the journal.

* * * * *

Con had sifted to meet with Aine. He hoped to get back before Em awoke because he'd forgotten to leave a note. He didn't want her to think he'd run out on her. But as usual, he got held up by the ridiculous pageantry of Aine's court.

First he'd had to wait as she heard from other advisors, then he'd had to fend off Ailish, Eire and Sorcha—all past lovers—none of whom were amenable to his turning down their offers of repeat erotic performances. It was nearly two hours before he finally got a private audience with Aine.

"What do you have for me, Con?"

"She knows I'm Fae and she knows I have more than a passing interest in her research. She wants to hear the whole story and I can only hold her off for so long. I'd like to tell her what I'm up to. I think she'll cooperate better that way."

"How does she know you're Fae and that you have more than a passing interest in her research, Con? Are you getting sloppy after ten thousand years?"

"She's a very clever human. She is also sister-in-law to a vampire I know. He told her who I was. I used my name and she found out that he knew me and asked him about me directly. The last time I saw this vampire was twenty-five years before she was even born."

Aine stood and walked around him, studying him carefully. "You have been with this human haven't you?"

"Yes. She's mine, Majesty."

Aine stilled and raised a brow. "Really? A human?"

He shrugged. He knew it was true, Em was his. But that also meant that he was hers and while he celebrated that it also made him uncomfortable. It had been a very long time since he'd allowed himself that level of vulnerability to another person.

"You are sure?"

"Aine, my queen, she's bound to my heart. I cannot imagine a life without her in it. Let me tell her the truth. Please."

"Your mother will be so pleased by this news," Aine said with a dry laugh. "Are you certain she can be trusted?"

He nodded. "Yes, she's got a pure soul. She is loyal and true. She would not use the book or any knowledge to cause harm."

"You may tell her that the symbol is related to Faerie magic and that we are concerned about the knowledge getting out and causing harm. Do not tell her more than she needs to know."

He inclined his head in thanks and deference.

He began to leave but she stopped him. "Conchobar?"

He looked up at her. "Yes, my queen?"

"I suppose this means you won't be making any trips to my bed again?"

He smiled sexily, his eyes twinkling. "I'm sorry to say so, but yes."

"I am sorry too. This human is a fortunate one to have your undivided attention. Many hearts will be broken and if I were you I'd be on the watch for spiteful females who may feel spurned."

"Thank you, Majesty. I will."

* * * * *

Bron MacAillen listened to the news of the discovery of the book with great interest. His father had looked for *The*

Shifting Veil for thousands of years to use against the humans. The magic in the book would allow him to break those ties that created protection from dark forces, leaving them vulnerable. Now, in supreme irony, a human had most likely discovered its whereabouts. A human whose family was the very key to him being able to get possession of the book once and for all.

He paid his spy and sifted from Tir na nOg to a place deep within the heart of the Forest of Infinity. He pulled out the dark book and spoke the ritual words, ending the spell with drops of his blood into the circle he'd erected.

The gagging stench of brimstone filled the air along with a sort of growl that made Bron's skin crawl and the hair on the back of his neck stand up. He had to fight against the urge to flee quickly from the presence of the demon lord he'd just summoned.

"Who are you and why have you summoned me?" the thing contained in the circle demanded of him.

"I am Bron MacAillen of the Dark Fae and I have a proposition for you."

"Why would I deal with you while you've contained me in this circle? Let me out and I'll listen to your story."

Bron laughed then. "If I let you out without a deal, it would be certain death for me. I have news that a book of very old Faerie magic, thought lost for millennia, may have been found."

"Why should I care? I loathe the Fae and their bright lights and urges to protect everything under the sky."

"Because this book contains magic that may be able to break the Compact that keeps you from destroying the human Charvez witches."

The demon narrowed his glowing sulphur green eyes at Bron. "Go on."

Bron went on to explain the chaotic magic within the book and the demon saw the significance of it right away.

"Faerie MacAillen, I think we must deal. Seal with me upon our mutual intent and you will remain unharmed but I will not work with you while captured like an insect within this circle."

And that very night, Bron took the demon's mark and entered into an agreement that would destroy the Compact that the demon was beholden to and the very man that Bron hated enough to summon a demon for.

Chapter Five

෨

Em wasn't in the penthouse when he sifted back. He grimaced when he saw it that was already evening. Time moved differently in Tir na nOg than it did in the human world. Her scent was there but cold—she hadn't been there in hours.

He frowned as he saw a paper with "Michael—two p.m.—Pig and Whistle, Oxford" written on it in a feminine hand. Who the hell was Michael?

He went to his suite but there was no message waiting for him from her. At least she hadn't gone through with her threat from the night before and had him kicked out of the hotel. He smiled wryly at the memory of how mad she had been at him. He still had no idea why she'd reacted so strongly to finding out he'd arranged to meet her.

Shaking his head to clear it, he thought he'd never understand human women as long as he lived—and he would live a hell of a long time.

Concentrating on her, he reached out and shimmered to where she was.

* * * * *

It was nearly two by the time she found the pub near Oxford that she'd arranged to meet Michael at. She saw him immediately as she entered. He was sitting at a table near the bar and waved at her.

She walked to him and he embraced her and kissed her cheek. "Em! You look lovely, darling. Sit down, I've got a pint for you." Michael Bertin had spent two years in New Orleans studying with her family and with other witches, wizards and sorcerers in the area. At nearly forty, he was quite the expert on most things magical and paranormal. He smiled at her and tipped his glass her way in a toast.

"Damn if you aren't a sight for these old eyes. You look lovelier each time I see you."

She rolled her eyes. "Old, my ass. You're what? Just forty? That's not old. A forty-year-old man is experienced enough to appreciate but young enough to have stamina." Em laughed and took a sip of the lager. "Hits the spot. Thanks."

"My pleasure. Now something tells me that this isn't just a social call." He looked at her curiously.

She felt his intense need to know things, to know everything. It was something about him that had always amazed her. She could feel his ease with her, his general happiness with his life and, oh, his sexual interest in the bartender. She had to dig her nails into her palm to not turn around to check him out again. She'd caught a big enough eyeful when she walked into the pub the first time. She had to agree that the hunky blond behind the bar was pretty delicious.

"Yes, I need your expertise, Michael. Shall we finish these and take a walk somewhere a bit more private?"

He turned serious and interested. "Sure. You've got my undivided attention."

They visited while they finished their beers then left the pub to walk the short bit to his apartment.

Once inside, she kicked off her shoes and sat on a big, overstuffed chair.

"Would you like a cup of tea?" he asked and she nodded. No one made tea like an Englishman. Before he left the room, he spoke under his breath and drew symbols in the air and Em felt the wards locking the bookshelves come open.

He bustled around the small kitchen as she looked over his bookshelves and coveted most of what she found there.

Ancient scrolls, books so old the leather was nearly dust, books in every language imaginable and several she'd never even seen before. "God, I want to cry every time I see a bookcase this juicy. Michael, you do have an amazing collection."

He came into the room and set the tray with the tea and cups and a plate of assorted cookies down on the coffee table. He came to stand behind her. "Thanks. Coming from you that's a real compliment. I hear you've added some of the books from George Carter's collection to your own. I'm jealous."

Her eyes lit up. "Oh, Michael. You should see these books! He has a complete set of the *Necromancer's Journals*. The spellbooks alone are priceless — evil and scary — but irreplaceable. You're welcome to see them any time. Alex, my brother-in-law and George's grandson, let me have unfettered access to the entire collection and gave me some exquisite pieces for the Charvez library. He's offered to make me the curator for the collection, which will be housed in Chicago. Of course, you have to know how pissed off that made the wizard community. They're not only sexist pigs but they believe that witches are inferior and having one with all of this access to the collection drives them nuts."

Michael laughed. "Well, they are an all-male society based on patrilineal power. One might guess that would breed a few sexists. Enough of this, as fascinating as it is. I want to hear why you're here."

He poured out and handed her a cup and saucer while she explained her research and the symbols she'd found in the margins of the journal. As his specialty was language, she hoped that he'd be able to give her some insight on the symbols. She was unable to contain her excitement as she told him about *The Shifting Veil*. Despite the seriousness of everything, she couldn't help but grin.

A look of pure wonder lit his face as he looked at the symbols and listened to her talk. "Em, I've heard about what I believe to be this book once or twice from the really old practitioners. Supposedly it's magic older than any other, more powerful than any other. If this book exists... Imagine the possibilities." He looked at her and grew somber. "Imagine the possibilities if someone or something on the dark path got this book..."

"Yes. It's why I'm looking for it myself. I want to get to it first, before anyone else does and uses it for evil."

He pulled out several of his most ancient books and scrolls and they pored over them for the next few hours. It was a disappointing experience. They found one reference to a book that had most likely been in a collection *The Shifting Veil* had been in at one time but nothing more.

* * * * *

She was sitting on the floor drinking a glass of wine, happily sated by an afternoon filled with research.

"I'm sorry we couldn't find anything. Will you let me know if you need help at Adelade's? I don't know that I could translate the book, I've seen that part of her collection before and was unable to figure any of it out, but I'd be willing to help in any way I can." Michael leaned in and raised a thumb to wipe a smudge of dirt from her cheek.

Con shimmered into the room and loomed over them, scowling. "And why are you touching her?" he growled.

Both Em and Michael jumped at his sudden appearance. Con grabbed Em and pulled her up to him, delivering a kiss so devastating that it made her nearly collapse in his arms.

"Did you not get enough last night that you couldn't wait until I returned?" he demanded.

Her brows shot up and the dreamy look of passion gave way to insulted fury. "What? Who do you think you are barging in here and making accusations? As if you had any right!"

"I'm your man, that's who I am. And you're my woman. If I didn't make that clear last night let me show you again—

over and over and over," he added, his voice going low and silky.

"Uh, hello?" Michael interrupted, holding out his hand to shake Con's. "I'm Michael Bertin, a friend of the Charvez family."

Despite her anger with Con, Em wanted to laugh at Michael's reaction. She could feel that he was near to bursting with curiosity about Con. He wanted to pelt the man with questions. He also wondered what Con looked like naked.

"Unbelievable," she murmured to Michael, answering his last unspoken question, but he didn't understand her meaning.

"Just being friendly. Wouldn't want him to get the wrong idea. He seems quite attached to you." Michael smirked.

"He's being incredibly rude!"

"He's in the damned room!" Con turned to Michael. "I am Conchobar MacNessa."

Michael's face turned pale. "*The* Conchobar MacNessa? You're Fae? The most honored of the Queen's Favored?"

Con nodded, looking down his nose arrogantly. He didn't want the other man to even begin to entertain the idea that he had a chance with Em. Em was his.

"It's an honor to meet you. I've studied your history. The story of the Thousand Year War... I've read odes written to your prowess on the battlefield. Do you have your magic sword with you? You negotiated the peace with the trolls and rode the Dark Fae into hiding. Simply amazing! I would love to interview you sometime. The history of the Sidhe is so fascinating. Do you live here among humans? What is Tir na nOg like? Do you travel through a dimensional rift? What is the source of your magic? How did you two..."

Em cut his stream of excited questions off. "He knows about the book but he's trying to pretend he doesn't. He lured me into a supposed chance meeting to try and find out what I was doing. He's here to make sure I don't find it without his knowledge."

"I'm here because you didn't leave a note as to your whereabouts and I was concerned," Con insisted.

"I'm a big girl! And you didn't leave a note before skulking out this morning either." The nerve of the man! Although, damn if he didn't look good enough to eat. He was wearing jeans that were fraying at the crotch and the pockets with a black crewneck sweater. Her mouth watered as she remembered what he looked like underneath the clothes.

"I don't skulk! I had a quick errand—or I thought it would be quick."

Michael cleared his throat and Con and Em ceased fighting and looked at him. Em blushed. "God, I'm so sorry. How crass of me. I apologize on behalf of Con for barging in here the way he did. I promise before I stop speaking to him entirely that I'll show him how to knock," Em said.

Michael laughed. It was good to see Em like this. She was the type to live in her head and it appeared that the legendary Faerie warrior was the man to get her out into the real world.

Con bowed. "I beg your pardon, Michael, I should have knocked. In my zeal to see Em again I lost my manners," he said insincerely. He'd just wanted to remind the other man that Em was his and that he was powerful enough to take care of any competition.

"Off with you then, Con. Michael and I were working before you popped in." She made a shooing motion with her hands.

Con insolently looked at the wineglasses and slid his gaze back to her face. "Is that so? Well, being ten thousand years old makes me a bit of an expert on a lot of things," he said with a bit of a leer. "I'm sure I can help with your work." He crossed his arms across his chest and Em's breath hitched as she watched his biceps bulge with the movement. Con caught her gaze, scented her wetness and gave a deadly, sexy grin.

"I, uh, think we were done, Em. You can go off now with Con, but I would truly love to speak with you, Con, about the

Sidhe and about your own history. You know, to see what's truth and what's exaggeration? We don't know a whole lot about the Fae really." He gulped in air and remembered Em. "You'll call me if you need help, right?"

She shot an annoyed glare at Con and then looked back to Michael with a smile. "I'll call you with whatever I find out." She kissed his cheeks and gave him a hug and turned, grabbed her bag and went to the door.

Con bowed to Michael, grabbed Em about the waist and shimmered them back to the penthouse.

She spun to face him, pulling out of his embrace. "How dare you!"

He leaned down and licked along the shell of her ear. She shivered. "Don't you try to use sex tricks on me, buster," she said faintly, quickly losing resolve.

"You're so beautiful when you're angry. It makes me want to rip your clothes off and take you against the wall."

"Oh?" She struggled as she lost the rest of her anger and began to think about how it would feel to have him take her against the wall. "You, you...you can't just barge into places and accuse me of being a slut!"

He stepped closer and she stepped back. "I would never call you any such thing. You're my woman, Em. I just got shaken to see you with another man like that. I would never hurl such hurtful epithets at you," he said, his voice smooth and thick.

She closed her eyes and took a deep, shuddering breath. "Another man? Michael is a family friend! He's not even interested in women! And what do you mean your...your woman? What are you talking about? We had sex. You wanted to know about the book."

His eyes flashed with anger and he stepped closer. She retreated, her back meeting the wall. "My woman. Mine. We had sex and, yes, I want to know about the book. The two things are not connected." His nimble fingers unbuttoned her blouse—pop, pop, pop. He bent his head and kissed the flesh that had been revealed. "I'm a very jealous man. I hadn't realized that until I saw you at the Lundi Gras celebration on the arm of another. I drove myself crazy thinking about you with him in bed, writhing underneath him. I almost shimmered into your apartment that night but I saw him walk away looking very disappointed."

"Lundi Gras? You were at Lundi Gras?" she asked, confused. His lips heated her flesh with each brushing kiss.

He slid the blouse off her arms and it pooled at her feet. "Mmm-hmm. I walked right by you. I had to touch you, smell you. I'd been dying to for weeks before that. Months. Of course that one small taste of you only made the craving worse."

He reached around and unhooked her bra and slid it off. Her head fell back and hit the wall but she didn't feel it as his hands slid up to cup her breasts, taking their weight, and his thumbs slid up and over her nipples. "I didn't see you. I know...ohh...I'd remember if I saw you."

He grinned as he dipped down to flick his tongue across the pebbled tip straining for his touch. Her hands had been motionless on his shoulders but now slid into the silk of his hair, pulling it over the bare flesh of her arms and torso, eyes closed as she luxuriated in that delicious texture.

"I was wearing a glamour. Blue eyes and black hair. You looked at my ass when I walked away," he said and went back to flicking his tongue over nipples begging for his touch.

"Oh! It was you? A fine ass it is too. You seemed so familiar then. I know now."

"Know what?"

"Nothing. You were going to tell me why you've been spying on me all this time?" She struggled to be stern but was losing that battle as his mouth moved over her heated flesh.

"That was part of my errand today. I wanted to get permission to talk to you about what I was doing." He unbuttoned her jeans and slowly brought the zipper down to reveal a pair of scarlet panties. "Very nice, red is my favorite color, you know," he said as he slipped two fingers inside them and found her very wet and ready pussy.

She made an incoherent sound and pushed herself into his touch. "So tell me. Oh god…that's so…oooh…"

Chuckling, he knelt and pushed her jeans to her thighs, effectively holding her legs tight. "Shall I tell you after? Or now? Or during?"

He stroked a middle finger through her wet folds, distributing her glistening honey over her pussy flesh, lubricating her as he moved. He gave the barest of touches to her clit and stroked down to push into her gate and up into her tight heat. "So fucking tight it makes me mad with longing," he whispered against her nipple.

She writhed, trying to widen her legs. "No, *mo fiach*. I don't want you to be able to move. Your pleasure is my job."

He looked up into her face. Her eyes were heavy-lidded and her lips glistened because she kept licking them, driving him even more insane. He stopped. She blinked and made a sound of distress.

"Shall I tell you now?"

"Don't stop!"

"Tell me what you want, Em."

"Keep on doing what you were doing," she begged.

He gave her clit a soft caress and then backed off. "Not good enough. What exactly do you want me to do to you, Em?"

She bit her lip and he swelled even tighter against the zipper of his jeans. She looked at him, clearly nervous. He drew a big circle around her clit never touching it. Instead, he used the flesh around it and the hood, caressing and tugging the flesh, creating wet friction that way. She whimpered and tried to move to get more but her jeans and his body held her in place.

"Oh, please make me come! Suck on my nipples, touch my…"

"Pussy? Cunt? Vagina? Slit?" he said suggestively, her emotional shift between wanton and innocent endearing her to him even more.

"Pussy. Please, Con. Fuck me with your fingers."

"As you wish, *a ghra*," he said and took her nipple into his mouth, sucking it hard as he slid his fingers back into her sheath. His other hand brought both breasts close together and he laved his tongue across both nipples as he fucked her with his fingers and flicked over her clit with his thumb.

She was so wet and hot, so responsive in his arms. His soul roared with possession and the need to mark her as his in some elemental way.

She mewled in the back of her throat as she approached her climax. The squelching sounds of his fingers buried in her flesh mixed with her moans and soft sighs. Her eyes fluttered closed and her lip was still caught between her teeth. Her fingers dug into his shoulders as he dipped down to feast on her breasts.

"Come for me, Em. Give yourself to me. I want your pleasure."

She writhed and bucked, clamping down on his fingers, coming with a surprised cry. Her cream gushed from her and rained over his hand, scalding him. Her clit bloomed under his thumb and pulsed in time with her clenching inner muscles.

"Yesss," she hissed in a long groan as she stiffened and then relaxed against his body.

He slowly pulled his hand out of her panties and picked her up, carrying her to the couch and pulling her jeans off, leaving her in those silky red panties.

"Thank you," she said dreamily as he ran his hands up her legs.

"Thank you, Em. It's such a pleasure to watch you fly apart in my arms." He stood, took off his sweater and tossed it to her. "Put this on or I'll be too distracted."

Of course, the sight of her in his sweater, her long legs naked, her face flushed, was more than distracting. It touched him in deep places he'd forgotten existed over the long years of his life.

"Distracted is bad?" she teased, running her hands up her torso and over her breasts. His cock threatened to burst through his zipper and cause him permanent damage.

"Stop that, minx. You wanted explanations. I'm going to give them to you and then I'm going to fuck you from behind." He put his arms across his chest and stood, feet apart in the stance of a warrior.

"Okay, but that," she motioned to him, "is also distracting. Stop it."

He grinned. "Tell me more. What specifically is distracting?"

"God, a ten-thousand-year-old legend fishing for compliments. Your biceps all bulgy and muscly, so sexy I can't stand it. Don't fold your arms like that. Just sit down."

He flexed his arms for her and quirked up a grin when her eyes widened at the sight. "Oh, all right." He sat down across from her. "First things first, we need to resolve this issue that you seem to have difficulty understanding. Let me be very specific so there is no misunderstanding this time."

He leaned forward and grabbed her chin and tipped it so that she was looking directly in his gorgeous golden eyes. "You are my woman, Em. You were meant for me and you know I was meant for you. I've been alive ten thousand years. There have been other women but never, ever, has a woman made me feel this way. You will not question this. You will not question why I am here, why I want you in my bed. These things simply are and you know that no matter how much you pretend not to." He kissed her softly, the barest brush of his lips against her own.

She looked at him and felt him inside her heart, in her soul. She wanted to believe him with all that she was but it was frightening to make the leap. She'd always imagined that when she fell in love it would be with someone she could read. That she'd have her gift to always know if what was between her and her husband was true. But she couldn't read Con. Could she take what he was saying on faith?

"Now that we've taken care of that, we can get on to the topic of the book. The book you're looking for is ours. You drew one of the symbols from it and it alerted my queen, who then sent me to watch you to see what your intentions were," he said simply.

"Ours? As in Faerie magic ours?"

"Yes. Does Adelade Belton have the book, Em? It's very important that it not go into the hands of the wrong person. Or any person for that matter. It needs to be returned to us before it can cause harm."

"Well, what the heck do you think I've been trying to do!" she exclaimed. "I'm trying to protect my family. Our power comes from a Compact. The power flows to us from that Compact in exchange for our protection of the innocents in our area. The magic in this book could dissolve that agreement and our power would be lost."

"So give me the book and I'll get it back to a safe place. I would never let you or your family come to harm. You're mine to protect now."

She stood up. "I don't have it! Why do you think I'm here?" She rolled her eyes as she began to pace. "You've been spying on me since January?"

"Yes."

"Oh my god! What do you think I am? Did you think I would use the book for some kind of nefarious activity? Why didn't you tell me sooner?"

"Why are you so upset? I knew pretty much from the start that you weren't going to use the book for evil but I was under orders from the queen not to reveal myself and to report back to her. I finally convinced her to let me speak with you and today I went to get her permission to tell you why I'd contacted you and why I wanted to know about the book. I didn't want any lies between us."

She threw up her hands and groaned in anguished confusion, walking to the doors that looked out over the city. It was overwhelming. It would have been confusing enough if he'd been a human man but this gorgeous specimen? Surely once he got what he came for he'd go back and she'd never see him again. She couldn't hold a ten-thousand-year-old immortal male! Faerie females were reputed to be great beauties with incredible magical power. She was an okay-looking empath, nothing special. She felt so far out of her league it made her dizzy.

"You're thinking again, Em. It's always troublesome when you do that. You work yourself up into some kind of state where you start to beat on yourself or me. Stop it. Believe in me, Em. Believe in yourself."

She took a deep breath and turned back to him. "I don't know how." She was quiet for a few moments and held up a hand to keep him back. She took a deep breath and forged on. "I'm supposed to go to Adelade's and look through her library. I think she has the book but doesn't know it. She's got a collection of books in dead languages that she's been unable to translate. I think the book is there. I was going to see if I could match the symbol to any of them. I'll just take you with me and you can have the book and take it back to wherever and I'll go home and the world will be safe for another season." Her heart stuttered at the thought of never seeing him again.

"Why do you doubt me, *a ghra*?" He wanted to shake her but he heard the doubt in her voice — the fear.

"I don't even know what I doubt. I don't understand this situation. I don't know what to do or say." Confused, she turned away and he caught her around the waist, pulling her into his body.

"You think I understand it?"

"Aidan told me that you were a womanizer."

He stiffened and for the first time in thousands of years felt embarrassment and regret over his behavior. He didn't understand it but he knew that the woman in his arms would be the only woman for him for the rest of his life. He'd waited all of his life for her and now that he had her there was simply no way he'd let her go.

He sighed and sat down, pulling her onto his lap and into the shelter of his body. "Em, I won't deny that there have been many women before you and that I have a reputation for being a great lover of women. But I object to the term womanizer. I never manipulated or hurt the women I was with.

"But that means nothing now. How can I convince you that you're the only woman I want? The only one I need?" He gentled his tone and touched her face.

"I don't know," she whispered softly. But she didn't care because at that moment, in his arms, she didn't want anything else. She'd figure out the rest later but for now she just wanted him to touch her.

"*A ghrá mo chroí*, let me show you with my body, prove to you with my touch," he whispered seductively as he nuzzled the place where her neck met her shoulder.

She sighed as she turned into his body to give him more access.

He felt a surge of triumph as she softened and surrendered to him. He drew off the sweater and turned her to face him astride his lap. "Your body is incredible," he murmured as he skimmed his lips across her collarbone and down the seductive curve of her breast. He curled his tongue around her nipple and she shuddered.

She reached between them to undo his pants but he grabbed her and held her wrists together at the small of her back.

"I want to touch you," she said, her words slightly slurred as he abraded her nipple with his teeth.

"You will. But for now, I plan to feast on you and I won't stop until I get my fill," he said in that musical voice that she'd come to love.

He used his free hand, sliding it down her neck and over the other breast, stopping to palm her nipple and then roll and tug on it until she arched into him, grinding her pussy over his lap.

"Take your hair down. I love the way it looks when it's unbound… The way it feels when it glides over my skin," she breathed out.

He looked into her face and reached back, removing the leather thong holding his hair back and it tumbled free. Her eyes closed at the intensity of feeling as the silky texture feathered over the skin of her arms.

"Wrap your legs about my waist," he ordered, still holding her wrists so that she couldn't move her arms.

She squirmed so that she could wrap her legs around him and he stood, carried her into the bedroom and deposited her on the bed. He stood over her, his golden eyes glittering with desire.

"So long and lithe. Sexy." He picked up her foot and massaged the arch, his big hands kneading. "Your legs do me in. I love long legs and every time I look at yours all I can think of is having them wrapped around my waist or thrown over my shoulders." He gave her a wicked grin and moved his hands up her calves. He knelt beside the bed and laved the backside of her knee and she gave a soft, breathy moan of pleasure.

He traced up the inside of her thighs with his fingertips, carefully skating over her pussy, up to the waistband of her panties. She watched as he drew them down her legs, tossing the scrap of silk to the side. He drew open her labia with his thumbs. "So pink and pretty, soft and," he leaned in and gave a long lick, "juicy. Knowing I'm the first, and the only man to ever be here and see this, touch this, taste this...it makes me hard. Makes me want to show you a hundred times a day just how good I can make you feel."

Em stared at Con, unable to speak around the lump in her throat. This man did things to her, thawed out her heart, made her feel desire. Desired.

She reached down and caressed his face, drawing him upwards, needing his lips on hers. When he kissed her she felt the last bit of the defensive wall she'd built around her heart shatter into a million pieces. She knew she'd been lying to herself that it was just about wanting him sexually. She admitted to herself then that she'd never be able to stop herself from loving him. That she already had loved him since before she'd ever met him.

He devoured her. Using lips, tongue and teeth he tasted every bit of her mouth. Their tongues slid seductively against each other, he sucked her bottom lip into his mouth, between his teeth. She tasted like innocence and seduction all at the same time, and of the red wine she'd been drinking. The faint smell of citrus rose from her skin as his touch heated her.

"I want you to be mine, Em. Will you give yourself to me?" he asked seductively, his lips against her ear as he kissed and bit along her neck.

"Yes," she said because there was no other answer.

He rubbed his face catlike along the inner curves of her cleavage. "I'm going to put my cock here and fuck your gorgeous breasts," he murmured and she whimpered. Hearing him talk that way made her feel deliciously naughty.

He bit and licked her nipples using the flat of his tongue, the sides and the tip until she was trembling on the knife edge of orgasm. He pulled his lips back and she made a sharp sound and pulled him back toward her.

"I'll bring you to climax, *a ghra*, but in my own way." He flipped her over onto her stomach and licked down the long line of her spine, swirling his tongue in each dimple at the base. He drew the tips of his fingers over her heated, sensitive flesh and she arched, opening herself to him.

"Your ass should have odes written to it," he murmured teasingly and bit one cheek and then the other. She pulled away from him and he pulled her right back. "Oh no, don't hold yourself away from me, Em. You said you'd give yourself to me, that you'd be mine. I mean to have every bit, body and soul." He drew back—she could feel his hair slide over her back and thighs. "Ass up in the air, *mo fiach*."

She did as he ordered and cried out as he pressed his face into her pussy. Growling, he pushed her thighs further apart. "Such a taste. Such a tight, hot pussy and all mine." He lapped at her swollen flesh, taking long licks, gathering her juice up, devouring her as if she were a ripe plum.

"Has any other man ever touched this pussy?" he growled at her.

"N-no," she moaned into her pillow as he traced the blunt pad of a middle finger over the rosette of her anus while slowly sliding a finger into her gate.

"Never? No hands, no lips or teeth?" he asked as he grazed her clit with the edge of his teeth, flicking across it with the tip of his tongue.

Her thighs began to tremble. "No!" She squeaked as he slid his thumb into her ass and pinched her perineum between thumb and forefinger.

"No?" he asked and drew back.

"Ack! Don't stop! I meant no—no one else has touched me but you," she cried out with frustration and pressed back toward him.

He chuckled wickedly and resumed his erotic devastation of her body.

"Has anyone but me ever made you come?"

"Yes."

He stopped and slapped one ass cheek sharply.

"Ow!" she cried out and the pain was replaced by a warm pleasure as he blew over the sting.

"Who?" he asked with deadly menace.

"Me..."

"Oh," he said as he slid another finger inside her and sucked her clit fully into his mouth.

Her eyes slid shut and she pressed her face into the pillow. She was unable to hold back a scream as her climax slammed into her body and every single nerve ending sparked to life and fried.

Before her body stopped spasming, he moved up and slid his cock into her. Her body stretched to accommodate his, welcoming him back with a tight squeeze of muscle. "Oooh...yesss," she groaned as he pushed into her wet heat. "I've never felt anything so good."

He stopped when he was seated completely inside her, his fingertips tracing the lines of her vertebrae, each rib, the curve of her back, the slope of her breasts.

"About that 'you making yourself come' thing," he said as he pulled nearly all the way out and pushed back in. Satiation stole over him, his eyes were heavy-lidded, muscles warm and lax. "We should talk about that in detail. I might need a demonstration or two."

She'd never felt so damned full in her life. His cock sliced through her. He had a slight curve and each inward stroke caused the fat head to brush across the bundle of nerves she thought only existed in books. Each pass over that sweet spot caused her such intense pleasure that it bordered on pain. She wanted to pull away from him at the same time that she ground herself back against him to get more.

Con was very close to losing control. She was so wet that her thighs were glistening with her honey, as were his thighs, and the heat of it scalded his balls. Still virgin-tight, her muscles clutched at him desperately, pushing him, begging him to slam into her over and over. It didn't help that she was thrusting that delicious ass back at him, grinding into each thrust and making erotic whimpers and mewls of pleasure deep in her throat.

Em could sense him holding back. She wanted all of him—he'd taken all of her and she wanted the same in return. "Don't hold back with me."

"I don't want to hurt you," he ground out around clenched teeth.

"Oh just fuck me already! I'll tell you if you hurt me." She pressed back at him hard. A juicy slap sounded through the room as their flesh met. "Please, give yourself to me, Con. All of you."

That last comment pushed the tatters of his control aside. He grabbed her hips to steady her and hold her still and he pulled nearly all of the way out. He teased her with his cock head until she was whimpering. Finally, as she begged for it, he slammed into her, bumping her cervix. She yelled out, not in pain but in pleasure.

The delirious pleasure her tight pussy walls created burned through him like a brand—she marked him from the inside out. He pistoned into her body, watching her breasts sway delectably with each thrust. She swiveled her hips when she met his downstroke and he moaned.

Her body was milking him, pulling his pleasure out of him, wringing him out. He reached around and lightly fluttered the tip of his finger over her clit. She shattered into a million stars as he took her over the edge yet again.

The tight clutch of her pussy was all he could take and he slammed into her as he came, her name a shout on his lips. He held her tight against him as he pulsed into her over and over.

Chapter Six

Her legs gave out first. She crumpled beneath him and he quickly rolled to the side and pulled her on top of him. Her hazel eyes met his. "Wow."

"I second that," he said with a laugh as he leaned in and kissed the tip of her nose. He smoothed his hands down her back to her bottom.

"So, getting back to you getting yourself off. What do you fantasize about when your fingers are buried deep inside your pussy? Hmmm?" His eyes had that glow about them that Em realized meant he was turned on.

She quirked up a smile. "Honestly?"

"Well, you can weave me a sexy story later with another scenario of your choosing but knowing you, I'm betting the truth is sexier."

"I fantasize about you."

He blinked at her. "You never touched yourself before yesterday?"

"Oh, of course I did! Jeez. I may have been a virgin but I wasn't dead."

"Then how did you fantasize about me before you met me?"

She sighed, deciding to tell him the truth. "I've been dreaming of you for what seems like forever. Of you doing all of this to me."

He stilled, his stroking fingers stopped and he looked at her intensely. "Are you serious?" Disbelief gave way to acceptance and overwhelmed joy. It made sense. The intensity and depth of his attraction to her, their deep connection—it was fated.

"Yes. When I met you yesterday you seemed so familiar and when you got rid of your glamour and I saw your hair and your true features, I realized you were my dream man." She touched the flesh of his chest, above his heart, with her lips. "I've been waiting for you, Con. You are the man I'm meant to be with. Never in my life had I felt desire except in my dreams and only when it was you."

He framed her face with his hands. "You do me such an honor, *a ghrá mo chroí*. Why didn't you tell me this before?"

"I was embarrassed. I didn't know if you'd be weirded out. And what on earth are you saying?"

He smiled. "You need never be embarrassed with me, I'm touched and proud to be your man and I am honored that you are my woman. As for my Gaelic, I called you 'my heart's beloved' because you are."

She blushed prettily. "Ah hraw?"

"*A ghra* means my love."

"You called me that last night."

"I've known for months now. It's been driving me crazy not being able to touch you. You have no idea how relieved I was when Aine allowed me to contact you. I understand now we were fated to meet. You were born for me to love."

"This can't be real. I keep on thinking that I'm going to wake up."

He slid her up his body and kissed her deeply. "This is real or I don't want to wake up. I don't know how we'll make the details work but we will. I'm not going away after we get the book."

"How? You're an immortal. You'll stay young while I get old and gray and die. Even before that, I can't really imagine you living in an apartment in New Orleans."

"We can work around your mortality. Fae and humans can be together. As for where we'd be, I think you'd love Tir na nOg. It's a beautiful island surrounded by clear blue waters and the weather is always mild. We can be there while it's winter here, I can take us anywhere at any time."

"Work around my mortality? What does that mean?" she struggled to focus as his curious fingertips skated down the cleft in her bottom, dipping between her thighs and through her still desire-swollen folds.

"There are ways to make a human immortal, spells and tinctures. They can only be made by the strongest of us. Namely Aine, the queen. If I asked her to do it, she would. Would you want her to do it, Em? Would you want to be at my side forever?" He rolled her over so that she was on her back and he loomed over her.

"Forever is an awfully long time, Con. What happens if you make me immortal and get tired of me?"

He nipped at her shoulder. "Have I not told you that you are my heart's beloved? I could find something new to love about you every day for the next ten thousand years. We are fated to be together. Your dreams, Em. Your dreams tell me that this feeling I've had of connection to you is something more than simple attraction. We are written in the Book, you were meant to trace that symbol, Aine was meant to send me to you, I was meant to find you."

"The Book? The book I'm looking for?"

"No. But it is among the oldest of our books, as is *The Shifting Veil*. The book I'm talking about is *The Book of the Tuatha De*. Only the most fortunate of us are fated to have our names there, and the names of our heart's other half. It's close to the human concept of soul mates. I never imagined that my name was there. You can't fight it, Em. Why even try?"

Putting aside her intense curiosity over the books Con was talking about, Em thought about the concept that they were somehow meant to be together. "Oh, I don't know," she said, confused. People didn't just meet someone and fall in love and want to be together for all time! Then again, her sister had. Twice. Her dreams weren't the same kind as Lee's of Aidan and Alex had been but she did have the gift of prophesy in her family line. Should she open herself up? Take the leap to be with the most incredible man she'd ever met—one that she loved and who professed to love her?

"Don't know what? Can you not feel how much I love you? Do I not please you? Think of the places we can go. We can live in your New Orleans, although I insist that we buy a home. Your apartment, while nice enough, is not large enough for two. I also have a preference for making love in the bathroom and as such we would need a large two-headed shower stall with benches, a deep whirlpool tub and a great many mirrors. Your bathroom is too small. We could also live in Tir na nOg. I have a large home there, right on the water."

He found his way down to a nipple and sucked it into his mouth.

"How do you know what my bathroom is like?" she squeaked out.

"I watched you shower many times," he said with a wicked grin.

"Oh you did, huh? Were you worried I'd find the book in the shower?" she asked with her eyebrow raised.

"No, I'm just a pervert that way." He laughed and she pushed him back against the bed and scrambled on top of him.

"You're so beautiful. I've never seen a man so beautiful before," she murmured as she put her face into the crook of his neck and inhaled. He was warm and sexy and smelled of the wild, of the outdoors—of sandalwood and musk and woodsmoke. She drew her tongue from neck to ear and he moaned softly. The taste of his skin seduced her senses. He didn't taste of salt and flesh but of magic and masculinity. It was more of a feeling than a taste.

She licked around the shell of his ear and nibbled on the small point at the top. He cried out and arched his back. She pulled back and looked into his face with a surprised grin. "Your ears are erogenous zones?"

He nodded and pushed her face back to it. She licked across that endearing little point and he moved restlessly beneath her. She dipped her tongue inside the well of his ear and sucked the lobe into her mouth, learning him and learning what made him feel good.

Her hands smoothed down the wall of his chest and over his pebbled nipples. She scooted down and flicked her tongue across one and then the other, moving back up to the other ear, feeling empowered by the groan she got in response. She found that he seemed to like tiny nips right on the top of the point followed by a quick flick with the tip of her tongue.

Growling, he picked her up and stood. She looked into his face, surprised, and the look he was wearing was one of such raw desire that it made her pussy clench. He backed her to the wall next to the triple-mirrored dressing area.

"Watch me while I fuck you," he ordered in a low voice, lining his cock up with her gate and sliding inside.

Looking down, she watched his cock disappear into her body and slowly pull out, slick with her cream. She watched as one of his golden hands grabbed her breast and kneaded, plucking the nipple and rolling it. She looked in the mirrors and watched his ass as he thrust into her, watched the muscles on his back ripple, his thighs tighten up. His hair swayed, covering his body as he moved, teasing her with glimpses of bare, muscled flesh.

She watched them, watched his face as she moved her mouth to his ear and nibbled. His lips parted and his eyes darkened to the color of whiskey.

"If you do much more of that this will be over before we get started." His voice was a throaty growl.

She bit down on the tip of his ear and sucked it into her mouth and he cried out, slamming into her, her back protected from hitting the wall by his arm around her waist. "Yes!" she cried out. "Fuck me hard and deep, Con."

"You asked for it, *mo fiach*," he replied and entered her hard and fast and to the root. She felt deliciously filled, dominated by his size as his body surrounded hers, invaded hers. His cock head brushed over her sweet spot and she tightened her vaginal muscles and gripped him.

"Yes, sweet Em, squeeze me," he murmured. He began to tremble as she traced along the shell of his other ear with her fingertip while her tongue lapped at his lobe. No human woman had ever found out just how sensitive his Faerie ears were, especially near the pointed tip, and Em's sweet tongue and fingers were pushing him over the edge.

He drove his cock into her flesh relentlessly while he slid one finger and then another into her rear passage, fucking her in tandem.

"Oh god, that feels so good," she groaned, her warm breath brushing across his ear.

Her pussy was so unbelievably tight, her anus so smooth and viselike, his cock twitched, wanting to forge that passage as well as the pussy it was burrowed into. He wanted to take her every way imaginable. He grinned, knowing without a doubt that he had the rest of time to find out every way possible to bring her pleasure.

"I'm going to fuck this tight little hole, Em. I'm going to stuff you full of my cock and make you beg for more."

She whimpered, her body beginning to shake, muscles jumping, one hand brushing over his ear, the other buried in his hair.

His strokes hammered into her body. She was covered in a sheen of sweat that made her skin glow. He licked across a shoulder and took her into himself, the taste of her exploding through his system. Her diamond-hard nipples brushed through the hair on his chest.

"Maybe I'll get a vibrator and work it into your pussy while I'm back there. Better yet, you can do it and I'll watch you while I'm buried balls-deep inside of your ass," he panted, his climax nearing. He adjusted her in his arms so that the length of his cock stroked over her clit with each thrust. He could feel that bundle of her pleasure, hard and swollen with desire, caressing his flesh on each pass. Her breath came in shallow pants and she was whimpering.

"Come for me, Em. Rain that sweet cream all over my cock," he murmured into her ear. She threw her head back and screamed out his name as her orgasm rolled over her, pulling her down and under the waves of pleasure. She drowned in sensation, her body alive with feeling, deaf and dumb to everything but the rush of passion he evoked.

He was a goner the moment she began to climax. Her pussy clutched at him greedily, sucking him back inside as she writhed in his arms. He stiffened as he pushed as far into her body as he could and felt as if his entire being was shooting through the head of his cock deep into her.

Minutes later, after leaning them both against the wall for support, he gently set her on the ground.

"You were worth the wait," she said, eyes alight with love.

He felt her words wrap around his heart and smiled. "We're going out to eat tonight. The Savoy, I think. Get dressed up, I'm going to arrange everything and I'll be back in an hour to escort you." He bowed low and shimmered out of the room.

* * * * *

After her shower, Em opened the closet to look for something to wear and was surprised by the ruby red dress hanging there. She reached in and pulled it out. It had hand-beaded spaghetti straps and a low, dipping bodice and was practically backless. It was also short. She looked at it skeptically. She'd never worn anything so blatantly sexy before in her life, usually sticking to jeans and longer skirts. The material caressed her skin as she looked at it. Well, she'd wanted to start showing the world that she wasn't some shy bookworm. She shrugged her shoulders and decided to go for it. After all, she was now involved with the most delicious man she'd ever seen—she needed to keep up.

She turned to find a tiny scrap of red lace that masqueraded as underwear on the bed and a pair of ultra-feminine stiletto heels on the floor next to it. She smiled goofily, Con had been a busy boy while she was showering. There was also a beaded bag to match the dress and a gorgeous pair of diamond chandelier earrings. For a warrior, the man certainly knew his fashion.

She did her makeup and hair and pulled on the dress, trying not to be nervous about the vast amount of skin showing. The shoes slipped on and she nearly gasped when she saw herself in the mirror. It was as if she'd become the woman she'd always been on the inside. The woman in the mirror was confident and sexy and well-bedded. Her hair was tousled, lips bee-stung and glossy red. The red of the dress set off the onyx darkness of her hair and the pale creaminess of her skin. Her legs looked miles long with the heels and her breasts looked quite lovely in the bodice of the dress.

She looked at the clock. She had fifteen minutes until Con was due to arrive. She called Adelade and made arrangements to come to her estate the next day, and also dialed Lee's. If she didn't return her call that night, Lee might just find it necessary to get on a plane and come interfere in person.

"Hello?" Lee's voice was sleepy.

"Hiya. Sorry to wake you, I am on my way out but I wanted to return your calls before you panicked."

"Ha ha. Why didn't you call me back earlier?"

"I was busy. I'm fine, having a great time. I saw Michael earlier today. He looks great and said to pass on his congratulations on your marriages."

"Busy doing what? Come on, I'm dying here! I talked to *Maman*, you know, she told me you'd met a man and by met, I think we all know she meant slept with. Is this the same guy you were with last night when you ditched me for Aidan and then hung up before I could ask any questions? The Faerie? Aidan says that he's quite the stud."

"Yes, that would be Con."

Lee exhaled with frustration. "Well, spill for goodness's sake! Jeez, I'm your sister, you need to tell me all of the naughty details. They are naughty, aren't they?"

Em took a deep breath, remembering each detail—and yes, they were naughty. "Mmmm-hmmm. Very, very naughty. He's really good at naughty."

Lee snorted with amusement. "So the dry spell is over, huh?"

"Yes. Over and over again."

Lee gave a delighted laugh. "I have got to meet the guy who finally got my baby sister into bed and made her sound so happy."

"You will. I will be accompanying Em back home to meet her family after we get married."

Both Em and Lee gasped. Em spun to see Con standing in the living room of the penthouse holding the phone extension. He was wearing a dark charcoal-gray suit, Prada, she'd guess by the cut and style. His hair was back and he had a glamour on his ears so the points weren't visible. He looked like walking sin. Her mouth dried up.

"Hey, this is a private call!" she said with a laugh.

"My ears were burning, *mo fiach*. I knew you were discussing me. I just wanted to be sure your representations were fair. Naughty indeed," he said, his voice low and filled with promises.

"Boy, I can't wait to meet this guy," Lee said and Em could hear the grin.

"Back off, you already have two," Em said. Hell, when Con got a load of Lee he'd probably regret that he'd met the wrong sister.

Lee laughed. "And two is more than enough for me. So, what's the plan for this wedding? *Maman* will have your head for doing it without family."

"Em and I will work it out and she'll let everyone know. It's all up to her, I am merely her servant in all things."

Em raised a brow at him and tried not to smile but failed. The man was irrepressible. "I haven't been asked to marry anyone so I'll get back to you after I am— and if I accept. We're late for our dinner date, Lee. Please kiss Alex and Aidan for me. I'll talk to you later." Em blew her sister a kiss and hung up quickly before Lee could ask any more questions.

Con put the receiver down and stalked toward Em, his eyes greedily taking in every inch of her. He'd seen the scarlet dress hanging in the window of the shop he'd shimmered into to get his suit. It looked even better on her than he'd imagined it would. He took in the shoes and the red-painted toenails. "We'll keep those on later when we get back," he growled as he circled her. He leaned down and kissed the small of her back. "You look good enough to eat. I don't know that I should let you out in public looking this spectacularly sexy. It's a good thing I'm a warrior—I'll have to fight men off all night."

She was speechless. He looked at her like he was a big bad wolf and she was a deer. Her nipples hardened, begging for his attention, and got it as he reached out and flicked an index finger across the peak.

"Shall we be going then, *a ghra*?" He held out an arm.

She nodded and took the proffered arm. He escorted her downstairs and into the waiting limo.

Chapter Seven

෨

They pulled up in front of the restaurant and Em gasped softly. From the perfect suit and shoes on the doorman and valet to the regal exterior, The Savoy was an impressive place.

"Good evening, Mr. MacNessa, Miss," the white-gloved doorman said as he handed them off to the hostess, who looked at Con like she wanted to throw him back on a table and climb aboard.

"Mr. MacNessa, how nice to see you again. You're my favorite customer," she cooed as she stroked his forearm.

Em took a deep breath, annoyed. Con, for his part, didn't even notice. "Yes. We'd like to be shown to our table now," he said without looking at skanky hostess girl. Em stifled the desire to stick her tongue out at the other woman after she'd handed them menus and sauntered away.

She looked around the room. It spoke of quiet, old-world elegance from the cut crystal stemware to the silver and gold-rimmed china at each place setting. The tablecloth was the finest linen and the candles smelled of sweet beeswax. The atmosphere was hushed and a string quartet was playing in the background.

"Will you trust me to order for us? A special meal?" he asked as he nibbled her fingers, bringing her attention back to him.

"Sure, I love everything but organ meats and brussels sprouts."

"I believe you like some organ meats," he said, voice silky with innuendo, and sucked her finger into his mouth.

She shifted in her chair, squeezing her thighs together, her pulse pounding. "Yes, but I wouldn't order that in a restaurant. There's only one distributor in town whose organ I like to eat and it's only good in the proper setting," she teased back.

He licked his lips and gave her a look that promised his organ would be on the menu later.

"Wine, Mr. MacNessa?" the female wine steward purred at him. She pushed between the two of them, shoving her tits in his face.

Con moved back and looked around the steward. "*A ghra,* would you like some wine?"

Em reached out and pushed the steward back so she could see Con without craning her neck. "Sure, but without the breasts please," she said with fake sweetness to the steward. Con put two fingers over his lips to stifle his smile. "You know what you're ordering so you pick the wine."

"Well, you know all of our specialties. Just ask and it's yours," the steward said to Con.

Em snorted and rolled her eyes.

Con ordered a nice Chilean red and looked back to Em. The steward flitted away. The waiter, thankfully male, took their order. Con relayed that he'd already spoken to the chef and had ordered ahead of time. The waiter couldn't take his eyes off Em's breasts as he nodded at what Con was saying.

"Son, those aren't on the menu," Con said with menace.

Em burst out laughing and the waiter blushed and excused himself.

"Why did I choose that dress? Men have been staring at your breasts since we arrived, looking at your legs, imagining them wrapped around their waists as they fuck you. From now on, you'll wear long skirts and baggy sweaters."

Em laughed and patted his hand. "Oh please! Every time anything with a vagina enters the room or gets near you, she has to rub her tits all over you and offer you sex in twelve ways! Anyway, I love this dress. I love how I feel in it. Where did you get it? My bills are small, I have a nice savings. I think I might make a side trip to wherever you got it and pick up a few more."

"Before *we* leave and you don't have to use your savings on anything. All you desire is at my fingertips. Just ask and it's yours. It brings me pleasure to spoil you."

"We'll see. I don't know that I like the idea of being a kept woman."

He threw back his head and laughed. "You'll be no such thing. You're my woman, my wife."

"About that…" But before she could say anything else the wine arrived and the steward and her breasts with it.

She stood there, licking her lips and bending over Con as he ignored her. "Lovely, thank you," he said of the wine, dismissing her.

The steward stayed. "Are you sure I can't get you anything else? Anything at all?"

"Hey, bimbolina, leave the wine and take your boobs! He's not interested!" Em hissed angrily.

The steward jumped and looked back at Em. She sniffed indignantly and stomped off.

Con poured her a glass of wine and handed it to her, wearing a badly suppressed grin of amusement. He touched his glass to hers. "To us, Emily and Conchobar."

She smiled at him and drank. The wine was rich and velvety and went down smoothly.

The food began to arrive and they both stopped talking for several minutes as they enjoyed the appetizer course. The entrée was a lovely mixture of grilled fish and steak. The vegetables were perfect and delicious. Con fed her bites of asparagus and salmon and she licked his fingers.

An hour and a half later, the table cleared but for a lovely slice of chocolate cake and a bowl of homemade ice cream, Con leaned forward and kissed her softly.

"This was lovely, Con. The best meal I've ever eaten."

"You haven't agreed to marry me."

She looked at him, one eyebrow raised. "You haven't asked."

He gestured with his head and she looked down and saw the small, black velvet ring box on the table in front of her. "Showoff," she said with a grin.

She cracked open the box and gasped. It wasn't some giant diamond that she would have been embarrassed to wear or a setting that was too lavish. It was an antique diamond ring in a platinum setting. In fact, she'd looked at this very ring every week for the last year as she passed by the jewelry store near her parents' house.

She looked up at him, tears shimmering in her eyes.

He leaned forward, alarmed. "I'm sorry, I thought you liked it, the way you looked at it..."

She put her finger over his lips and shook her head. "I love it, Con. These are good tears."

"So you'll marry me by human law as well as being my wife according to the laws of the Sidhe?"

She nodded and he smiled, relieved, and reached out to put the ring on her finger. She looked at it, glittering in the light of the candles in the room.

"We should get this cake to go. I can think of a better place to eat it," she said suggestively.

"Back in the penthouse?"

"Off your belly."

He made a gesture and the server quickly approached. "We'd like the whole cake to take away with us," he told the server and Em pursed her lips at him, taking his measure.

She excused herself to go to the ladies' room. Minutes later, as she returned to the table, she saw yet another woman had not only approached their table but was actually sitting in her chair! The woman was leaning toward Con, a hand on his arm. Em walked back to their table and watched as he smiled and flirted with the woman, laughing with her and making no move to remove the hand.

She came to a stop next to the table and looked down at the scene with a raised brow. "Excuse me, but we're on our way out to have some hot sex and eat cake off each others' naked bodies," Em said through a fake smile.

Con looked up at her and saw the dangerous glint in her eye. He stood up smoothly, nodded to the other woman briefly and turned to Em. "I've got the cake right here, *a ghra*. I've been waiting most anxiously."

"Mmmm-hmmm," she said with a glint in her eye and took the arm he'd been offering. They walked out of the restaurant and he helped her into the limo.

"I sense that you are a bit miffed with me, Em," he purred at her as he kissed each of her fingertips.

Em looked at him and snorted, remaining silent for the ride, working through her feelings. He had ignored the steward and the hostess but she hated that other women constantly seemed to throw themselves at him.

He was so incredibly handsome that it made her feel a bit insecure. Yet she was wearing the ring he'd given her when he'd proposed to her not a half hour prior. She had to face her insecurities about not being able to read him. Other people did it every day, didn't they?

Con watched her as they drove, holding her hand in his own. He could feel that she was thinking about something and he was a bit uneasy about it, but she didn't seem panicked and hadn't removed her hand from his and so he tried to give her the silence she seemed to need.

Back at the hotel he picked her up and stalked into the bedroom, tossing her on the bed and immediately covering her body with his own. "Tell me."

She looked up into his face. He'd shaken off the glamour as soon as they'd walked in the door and features that were as familiar to her as her very own greeted her. "I don't like the other women," she said, feeling totally stupid as she said it.

"What other women?"

"Everywhere we go there are other women. And when I came back from the bathroom there was another woman sitting in my chair, with her hand on you, and you were flirting with her and it just made me feel a bit insecure for a moment."

He kissed her hard then, not stopping until he felt her anger begin to melt. "Yes, women flirt with me and yes, it does amuse me. I'm flattered, sometimes I'm annoyed. Sometimes I flirt back. But it means nothing. None of them can compare to you. Em, women do look and offer, it's something that happens frequently. But I'd never take them up on it. You know that, don't you?"

She looked at him and knew the answer, even without her gift. It was in the way he held her, the way his weight was on her but he held himself up with his arms so he wasn't on her totally, the way he touched her and looked at her. "Yeah, I guess I do. I just…never mind. I was being stupid and feeling possessive. You're the first and only man I've ever loved. I just feel a bit out of my depth with you sometimes."

"You love me?" he asked, wearing a stupid grin.

She slugged his shoulder. "I said I'd marry you, didn't I?"

"Yes, but you hadn't said you loved me." Con's heart felt close to bursting at the words from her—his Em loved him.

"I told you that I'd been waiting to give myself to you since I first started dreaming of you. You're truly the man of my dreams."

He brushed her tears away with his thumb. "*Is tusa mo shaol*, you are my world, Em. My life. No other woman has held a place in my heart but you. The flirting means nothing but if it hurts you, I will stop. Never doubt the way I feel about you," he said softly but clearly as he reached beneath her dress and pulled her panties off. "You're wet for me, Em." His whiskey eyes saw through to her very soul and all she could manage was a nod.

Reaching down, he unzipped his suit pants and freed his cock. He pulled her to the edge of the bed and plunged into her wet heat and began to drive her slowly toward climax. "Only you, only you, only you…" he chanted over and over as he thrust into her body.

Chapter Eight

ဆ

The wakeup call came much too early the next day. Em blearily grabbed the phone and then hung it up. She started to roll out of bed but an arm banded around her waist and dragged her back.

"Where do you think you're going?" Con growled sleepily.

She grinned at him even as her body began to respond to him, to his scent and to the feel of his arm against her body. "To Adelade's. She's expecting me — us, if you want — for lunch and letting me into her library." She nuzzled into his body, his warmth too hard to resist.

"Do we have to go just yet?" he asked seductively.

"Oh no, we don't have time for that," she scrambled out of bed but he caught her, pulling her down to the mattress again. She laughed, realizing that she hadn't been so relaxed in a very long time. Her ring winked in the morning light and she held up her hand to look at it better.

"Ah, now you act like a stereotypical engaged human female," he said smugly.

She raised an eyebrow at him. "It is beautiful and I do love it. It's very sweet of you to have noticed me looking at it." That touched her deeply, knowing that he'd really thought about what she liked. What mattered to her mattered to him.

"I know a way you could show your appreciation," he said suggestively, waggling his eyebrows.

She writhed underneath him and they both made soft moans of pleasure at the contact. "We really don't have time. Adelade lives outside of London and we should leave in about twenty minutes to get there on time." She said it but there wasn't a lot of conviction in her voice.

He opened his lips and skimmed his way down her neck, feasting on her frantic pulse. "You forget that all I need to do is wish us there and we'll be there in the blink of an eye. We have plenty of time." His hand slid up her thigh.

"I need to take a shower. Faeries may not sweat but humans who've had sex all night long do." She was slightly put out when she said it—how could a man work as hard as he had over the long, erotic hours they'd spent in bed the night before and not get sweaty?

"Okay. I'm a very versatile man and I'm aware that we haven't had shower sex, which, I have told you, is one of my favorite things."

"Until I met you chocolate was my favorite thing," she said with a grin. Yeah, this trip was really, really good so far.

Chuckling, he stood up and pulled her to her feet, dragging her into the bathroom.

Once under the hot spray—and Em did have to admit that double-headed shower stalls were the coolest thing ever— he soaped her up, his hands gliding over her slick body, taking inventory of each dip, each fold, each curve and line.

"Put your hands, palm flat, against the tile and spread your legs," he ordered in her ear.

Pulse racing, she turned to face the tiled wall and put her hands as instructed. She reflected for a small moment that this was totally out of character for her. She was an exceptionally responsible person. She didn't show up late to things because she had to fit in a quickie! But, he could get them to Adelade's with magic and this man just flat out eroded all of her willpower. And she liked it. It wasn't that she was a different person. He hadn't changed her so much as unlocked the sensual, sexy woman who'd always been inside her just waiting for the right man to inspire her.

There, hands flat against the tile, a big gorgeous man behind her, his hands all over her, she felt like a goddess. A siren. He made her want. He made her *need*.

She eagerly complied when he pushed her legs open wider with his knee and grabbed her hip, tilting her ass out and up. His soapy hand was caressing her breasts, kneading, tugging, pinching and stroking. Her pussy was molten and empty.

He teased her with his body. His cock stroked almost casually between the soap-slicked globes of her ass. His torso caged her in delicious dominance and each tug on her nipples shot straight to her clit. She was nearly sobbing with her need for him.

"Please, Con, I need you inside of me," she said softly, yearning in her voice.

"Is that so, *mo fiach?*" he said, his voice like sin in her ear. He continued his devastation of her body, each touch making her more his woman, each nuzzle and kiss branding her.

"Yes!" she cried out, arching her ass back toward him.

With an amused chuckle he bent to adjust for their height differences and began the inexorable press of his body into her own. She was unable to stop a long groan of satisfaction and she tilted back further to meet his thrust. "So good, you feel so good," he rumbled into her ear.

"More," she whispered. "Con, please give me more." If she'd thought on it more she probably would have been embarrassed but she felt fearless with him.

"Yes, *a ghra*, yes. Take more," he said and took her earlobe between his teeth. He fucked her slowly and thoroughly, the hot water pelting down on them, warming skin and loosening muscles. His hand, slowly stroking her clit, brought her to climax as she writhed against him, trying at once to escape the pleasure and get the most out of it that she could. He did this to her twice more before he finally allowed his own orgasm.

The thrust deep within her once, twice, three times. With each stroke, she could feel the pulse of his cock as he came.

He rinsed her off as he kissed her neck. "I've created a monster, haven't I?"

She smirked at him — he had *no* idea — and went into the bedroom to get dressed. She opened the underwear drawer and let out a surprised gasp. There was a rainbow of silky panties just waiting to be worn. Pulling out a silky, midnight blue thong, she looked at Con with her eyebrow raised in question.

He smiled without a bit of guilt. "Delightful, aren't they? I was walking past this lovely lingerie shop and saw them. I thought they'd suit you — they certainly did last night."

"Where are my old underwear?"

"Oh, around. You can see that I left the sexy pairs you already had. As for the plain cotton, well, they're perfectly lovely, Em, but I thought you'd appreciate some new ones. Sexy and silky, just like you." He practically batted his eyebrows at her.

"Look, Eddie Haskell, I appreciate the gift and all but you can't just throw away my panties without asking." She slid the silky blue thong on and it did feel very nice against her flesh. Her normal undies were cotton, functional and comfortable. Functional and comfortable were good things, she thought to herself as she spied how sexy she looked and suppressed a smile.

"Eddie Haskell? Is that a former boyfriend?"

She rolled her eyes. "No, I don't suppose they have reruns of *Leave it to Beaver* in faerieland. It's a cultural reference, never mind. I just called you a kiss-up in a really witty way but it went over your head."

He looked mildly affronted by the faerieland comment but was much more interested in watching her ass as she went to the closet to pull out clothes. He handed her a midnight blue silk demi-bra. "This goes with the thong. I'm pretty sure it's your size."

She burst out laughing and tiptoed to kiss his lips. "Incorrigible. I won't even ask how you knew my bra size by sight and feel." She put the bra on and pulled a sweater on over it and decided to go with the black wool skirt with the kick pleat and the boots she'd bought.

"It's a gift," he said with an arrogant smirk. "Very nice. Snug sweaters with breasts like yours, mmmmm, makes my mouth water, Em. Love the skirt too, hugs your spectacular ass. And the spike-heel boots? Every man's dream. Promise to wear them later when we return? Just them—maybe with a flogger." He waggled his brows again and she just snorted.

"Are you getting dressed or not? We need to get to Adelade's—we should be meeting her there right now."

He sighed and suddenly was wearing a soft cashmere sweater and khaki pants. She looked down at the Gucci loafers on his feet and shook her head. "Do you just make the clothes up out of magic? I love designer clothes. Too bad I can't learn that spell."

He pulled her to his body. "But I know the spell. Anything you desire, Em, all you have to do is ask."

She looked into his eyes with amusement and affection. "You'll do, I suppose. Now let's go."

* * * * *

In the blink of an eye they were standing at Adelade's front door. Con reached out and knocked and Adelade opened the door herself moments later.

"Ahh! You've brought the handsome young Mr. MacNessa! Please, come in both of you. Lunch is ready."

Em pressed a kiss to the older woman's cheek and Con bent low and placed a courtly kiss on her knuckles. Adelade blushed and waved them inside.

Con held out his arm and escorted Adelade into the lovely dining room.

After he helped her into her seat he tossed an annoyed look at Em, who'd seated herself. "What?" she asked.

"You should have waited for me."

"For what?"

"To pull out your chair."

She sighed. "Oh good grief, Con. I'm perfectly capable of sitting down to eat. I've been managing it myself for over two decades now. I don't need a man to do it for me."

He sat in his chair and scowled. "But I wanted to."

"Don't pout, there are other things you can do for me," she whispered as Adelade spoke to the maid and asked to have lunch served.

His eyes twinkled and he looked appeased.

"My, don't the two of you look cozy. I take it the drink after dinner went well?" Adelade said, a twinkle in her eye.

"She's agreed to marry me."

"Oh my, ten thousand years of gallivanting must have made you sure when you found the right woman," Adelade said dryly.

"You know about me?"

"That you are the Conchobar MacNessa of Faerie legend? One of the legendary Faerie warriors that guards and counsels the queen? Of course I did, I wouldn't have left Em with just anyone. You do know that Em is a great empath?"

He turned to Em. "I knew she had talent and could read feelings. It's obvious that she's special."

Em smiled at the way he said it so proudly. "You haven't met the truly special women in my family yet. My gift is nothing compared to my sister's and my mother's, and my *grandmere* is a great seer with great prophetic talent."

Con's heart hurt to hear the self-deprecating words from her. Could it be that she truly didn't see her own gift as important? It wasn't that he didn't hear her pride in her family. Clearly she didn't feel jealousy or resentment about being in a family with other powerful witches, but it did seem to him that she saw herself, her gift, as less than those of the other Charvez women.

Adelade saw the self-doubt as well and sought to confront and correct it. "Yes, the power and skill of the Charvez women is legendary. However, you seem to underestimate your incredible gifts. You're not just an empath, but you possess an amazing ability to use intuitiveness in your research. I believe that this incredible gift of intuition comes from your grandmother's gift of foresight. You're one of the magical world's most renowned researchers and you're still so young. By the time you're my age you'll be legendary."

Adelade was glad she'd followed her instincts and let the Faerie press his suit with Em. Adelade had seen the way the man's eyes had taken in every detail of Em's face and mannerisms that first meeting and she'd thought that a big, bold man like Conchobar MacNessa would be a nice match for Em. Em, who many thought shy and bookish, but who was really just quiet and smart. Em was the kind of woman who *listened* before talking. Adelade respected that quality a great deal.

And Adelade knew of the seductive power of Fae males. Once upon a time she'd learned that firsthand. She just hoped it would have better results for Em and Con.

They ate a light lunch and Adelade showed them both into the library. When Em caught sight of the floor-to-ceiling shelves crammed with books of all shapes and sizes she gave a delighted squeal. Her eyes widened and she greedily took in row after row of books in the massive room.

Adelade looked at Em, pride showing on her face. "It is amazing, isn't it?"

"Amazing doesn't do it justice. Adelade, this library is better than chocolate. If I could live in this library I'd never leave."

Adelade gave a laugh. "Thank you, dear. You should consider yourself invited to visit it at any time. Shall we go on through to the unidentified collection, or the UWB—unidentified written book section?"

Con laughed as he watched the two women wax rhapsodic about the books. He was impressed. For a collection owned by a human it was quite comprehensive. He could feel the magic in the air.

Adelade led them into a side room and Con felt the book at once. As a magical being, he could feel the mixture of very old magic in the room. It swirled around him like the tide. Each kind of magic gave off its own rhythm, its own flavor. Con could discern their different energies. As he mentally searched through this stream of magical information, he found it in short work. Faerie magic gave off a very distinct feel, one that flowed through his veins. It resonated with him, clicked with his senses. He said nothing, not wanting to alert Adelade. He felt like he could trust the woman but he wasn't going to take any chances.

"Here we are. I'll leave it to you to decide where to start. I'm guessing that having Con with you will be your ace in the hole—not too many scholars have the depth of experience that he has. I've got to run out to a meeting of my charitable organization but I'll be back in three or so hours. If you need anything just ask my household manager. I've instructed her to make everything you need available." Adelade gave Em a quick kiss on the cheek and was off.

He waited until he heard her leave the house and turned his attention back to Em, who was walking through the room with a dreamy look on her face, running fingertips over the spines of the books. He smiled as he watched her—her love for the books was endearing.

"*A ghra*, you look so happy I feel jealous," he teased.

118

She turned and gave him a smile so beatific that he nearly gasped. "These books have nothing on you, Con, but they are so beautiful, aren't they? Imagine, witches and other magical folk writing down their Craft for thousands of years in thousands of languages. Each book is a part of them. Even though we can't understand the languages anymore they are still alive through the pages."

"I never thought of it like that but you're right." He kissed her temple and closed his eyes. He reached out with his power and turned as the Fae magic in the book called to his own. He walked over to a far shelf, slid an innocuous-looking tome out and sighed.

Em hurried over and peered at it. "Is that it?"

He nodded. "I need to take it back to the queen now, Em. I'll take you back to the hotel first," he said as he grasped her hand. Suddenly she was back in the penthouse.

"I'll be back when I can. It might be a while—time passes differently in Tir na nOg. I'm going to speak to the queen about you and when I get back we can discuss everything." He kissed her lips and was gone before she could reply.

Chapter Nine

ഔ

Con stalked into the queen's private audience chamber and got to one knee. Holding out the book he looked into her eyes, "Here is the book, Majesty. Safe."

Aine smiled at him and took the book. "I knew you would not fail me. Not once in all of these millennia have you failed a task. Sidhe and humankind alike are safer now that this is back with us." She waved at him to stand. "I take it you had no problems with the human woman?"

"She did not want the book for herself, she wanted to keep it out of hands that could harm her family. She did not argue with my bringing it back here."

"Good. Thank you for your service, Conchobar. Is there a boon you wish in return?"

"Yes. The human woman, I am in love with her. I wish you to administer the spell of immortality upon her."

Aine raised one beautiful golden eyebrow. She'd thought that this was where he was headed when he'd come to her before but she needed him to be absolutely sure. "I have not used that spell in three thousand years. Are you sure this human deserves it? Are you sure you love her, Con? Once she is brought over you know she'll need someone to show her all she needs to know. Are you going to be the one to show her how to wield her powers, to inform her of our rules and customs? You simply cannot walk away once you've tired of her."

"Majesty," he looked into her sky-blue eyes, "Aine, this woman is my heart. I knew it as I watched her for you. I knew it the first time I bedded her." He looked down at his hands a moment and smiled. "No, I knew it before that. I knew it as I watched her cooking and working in her family's shop and going about her human life. She has embedded herself in my soul. I feel her when I breathe, when I laugh or am sad. She is my first thought upon waking and my last as I fall into sleep. I will never be tired of Emily Charvez."

Aine's laugh was musical and seductive. "I never thought that you would be one for love. But I am so very glad you have found your fated one. You're giving up a lot, you know. Once you take those vows and the ceremony is finished, you're bound to each other for as long as the two of you are alive."

He nodded solemnly. "There've been thousands of women over thousands of years, I've been infatuated and loved many. I've never been in love with a single one. Em is my match and it's all the more sweet that it took ten millennia to find her. She is of pure heart and soul, Aine. She will carry her power with honor. I will see to her tutoring in our ways."

Aine inclined her head to him. "I loved someone once. He was my other half, but I was foolish and my mistakes led him to another and I lost him forever. Hold onto this woman if you love her, Con. Bring her to me and I will do this for you."

"Thank you, old friend."

She waved him off with a dainty hand. Laughing, he turned and left to seek out his brother and mother.

* * * * *

Bron sat up in his bed, the shock of magic arcing up his spine signaling that the book had been returned to its proper place.

Even though it had been lost, it was tied to all of them — to all Fae including the exiled Dark Fae. He had no doubt that others felt something at that moment too, although he doubted they'd understand the importance of it.

He snorted derisively. Those Fae that Aine ruled had no idea what power they all had. Or if they did, they had no real grasp of just exactly what they could do with it. No, they lived here and obeyed the Concordat. They rejected their immense power and left the humans alone or worse, protected them.

It was an offense against the oldest ones to kowtow to the weaklings called humans. Bron's father knew what it was to live up to their full potential as a species. He refused to obey the Concordat, instead, living as a Faerie should. They were immortals, gods! They were not meant to protect humans. Humans were nothing!

And yet, it was humans who got his father executed and Bron would never let that go unpunished. Humanity was a pathetic plague on their plane of existence. Their weakness and whining to the Fae like Aine got Aillen killed and Bron would not rest until Aine no longer sat on the throne, Conchobar MacNessa was with his father and humanity was enslaved to whatever future the demon lord had in store for them.

After Bron had made his deal with the demon lord, he'd continued the negotiations with the Fae. It was easier to fake it all without Conchobar's presence. Jayce MacTavish was a problem but at least Bron could be in the same room with him without wanting to kill him.

He'd worked with the rest of the Dark Fae, both those hidden within the ruling Fae and the ones who'd been exiled, to get their plans in place. Once Bron got that book to the demon lord and the human witches were felled and he'd destroyed the queen and her most trusted Councilor they'd move and they'd install their own queen on the throne.

With a triumphant smile, he smoothed a hand down the front of his shirt and set off to find his spy within the Court and then to seek out the demon.

* * * * *

"Finn!" Con called out as he approached the home in the middle of the forest where his brother and sister-in-law lived. He saw Finn on the shores of the lake playing with his three young sons. Cara, Con's golden lab was swimming with a stick in his mouth.

Finn looked up and grinned. "Con!" He strode toward his brother and took him into a crushing hug, slapping his back. "It is good to see you. What brings you to our home?"

"I have come to tell you of my new wife."

Finn's eyes widened and he began to laugh. "The human you were watching?" His arms were wrapped around his ribs he was laughing so hard. Cara ran around them all barking and shaking out her coat.

"What's so funny?" A curvy woman with a head of blonde curls came down the slope toward them wearing a wide smile.

"Magda, my darling sister. How are you?" Con asked, kissing her square on the mouth just to tease his brother.

"Con is in love, Mag m'dear," Finn said laughing as he scooped his wife away from Con's grasp.

Magda smiled and reached around her husband to hug Con. "That's wonderful! She must be an amazing woman to snare you. Is she the human you were watching for the queen?"

Con smiled, thinking of Em. "Yes. Her name is Emily Charvez. She comes from a family of powerful witches. She's a feeler and a scholar. Hair as dark as a raven's wing and hazel green eyes. She's tall for a human, lithe. Quiet, but strong. You'll love her, Mag."

"Of course we will. When do we meet her?"

"The queen has agreed to give her immortality. I'm going back to make plans with her. She's very close with her family and I expect I will meet them. I'll bring her back here as soon as I can."

"You'll have the Joining ceremony here, right on the lake. Your mother and I will grow flowers so thick they will be a carpet under your new bride's feet. Have you told her yet?"

Magda asked with some trepidation. Titania was not an easy woman and she had a very low opinion of humans.

"I came here first. I thought she might be here visiting the boys." Con watched his nephews splash about in the water like fish.

"She has been on the western shore for the last while," Finn said, a line of concern between his eyes. "She won't take it well but she'll get over it soon enough."

Con had been hoping his mother was with her grandsons, it made her more mellow. She was a grand lady but a terrible snob. Knowing that Em was not only lacking regal Faerie bloodlines but human too would definitely not make her happy. Underneath all of that though, she loved her sons and would come around and happily take Em into their family...eventually.

He allowed himself to be talked into staying for a meal with his brother's family to delay the inevitable.

* * * * *

The sun had set when Con shimmered in front of his mother's home on the western shores. She was sitting on a chaise lounge looking out over the sea and noticed him standing there. She stood up with a happy cry and came down the steps to greet her youngest son. The lavender-hued dress she was wearing fluttered against her golden skin in the sea breeze.

"Conchobar! My darling boy, I've missed you so!" She gathered him into a hug and kissed his cheeks. "You look well. Relaxed, even. I take it you are finished with your latest job for Aine?" She wrinkled her nose in distaste. "Imagine sending you to watch a human! Any old Faerie could have gone but she sent you!"

Con laughed and led her back to the chaise she had been seated on earlier. Titania was a small woman. She had golden blonde hair that she kept in an upsweep at the nape of her neck but Con knew that it shimmered in a river of gold long past her waist. When he was younger he'd watch her brush it out every night. Her eyes were the clear blue of the summer sky. She had regal features—high cheekbones and perfect rosebud lips. Hers was one of the most regal Houses of the Fae.

He created a goblet and poured himself some of the fruit nectar she'd been drinking and sat down across from her.

"Mother, I've got wonderful news."

"Yes, darling?"

"I've found my fated one."

Titania smiled and grasped his hands. "Oh, my darling! How fabulous. Who is she? What family is she from?"

"Her name is Emily Charvez and she's a witch. She lives in New Orleans in the human realm."

His mother paled. "A human? You must be joking, Con! You can't join with a human! You descend from the kings of old!" She stood up and crossed her arms. "I won't have it. You will not sully our bloodlines with a human, Con."

He checked his anger and took a steadying breath. "Mother, she is more than worthy. You'll love her once you give her a chance."

"I'll do no such thing! Conchobar MacNessa, what would your father say if he were with us?" Her hands waved about. "You're just confused. You've never settled for one woman for longer than a few months, here and there over the years. Once or twice a few years. She's a passing fancy. By the time you decide to sift back she'll be old and gray and you'll move on."

He stood. "Mother, I will not move on. Don't you think that after all of this time I know the difference between a passing fancy and my wife? She and I are fated, look into my heart and you'll see her there."

She spun and did just that. As his mother, she could see right into him. This woman was not only in her son's heart but in his soul, wrapped around him like tiny brilliant strands of golden thread. Their connection had healed old hurts, made him stronger, fulfilled him. She couldn't argue against that. Couldn't stand in the way of any woman, Fae or not, who made her son so beautiful inside.

She sighed and sat. "I see. Well, one can't fight fate. Bring her back to us. You have my blessing and I'll be honored to welcome this human into our family. I assume you've asked Aine to bring her over?"

"Yes and she agreed."

"As well she should. You've served her well and faithfully for millennia haven't you?" his mother sniffed. She'd never thought that slut Aine was good enough to be queen. "You'll stay the night with me. I'm sure your Em won't begrudge a mother a few precious hours with her son."

He stifled the urge to laugh at his mother's dramatics. "Of course, Mother."

Chapter Ten

ဢ

After he'd spent the next morning and early afternoon with his mother he sifted back to the penthouse, but it was empty. Em's scent was there but very faint. He walked about the rooms but they were empty except for the diamond earrings he'd given her that had been laid on the bed.

A sinking feeling hit his gut. He shimmered to the newsstand and saw on the front page of the *Guardian* that it was September. Three months had passed here in the human realm since he'd been home in Tir na nOg!

Cursing, he shimmered to New Orleans, right into her flat, and saw her sitting, looking out of the window. Her normally messy apartment was dirty. Dishes were piled in the sink and takeout cartons were all over the place. He watched her take a sip from a mug. It smelled like she was drinking herbal tea.

"What are you drinking, *mo fiach*?" he asked softly.

She turned so quickly she fell out of her chair. "*You*! How dare you!" She threw her mug at him. "You fucking Faerie bastard!" She battled her intense joy at seeing him and her fury that he'd been gone so long while she'd endured so much.

He deflected the mug and walked to her and smelled the despair seeping out of her pores. "Em, *a ghra*, I'm sorry it took me so long."

"You've been gone for MONTHS! Do you think you can just walk in and out of my life like that? Where the hell have you been?"

"I told you time moves differently in Tir na nOg. I was only there for a day and a half, I had no idea that so much time had passed here."

She tossed a plate at his head and he growled at her. "You asshole! Did you just growl at me?" She snorted in disbelief. She wanted to run into his arms and weep for joy but she was afraid to believe that he was really there.

"I waited for you for another week, and another. My family told me to come home, that you'd abandoned me. I told them that you loved me, that you wouldn't do that. After a month Lee and Alex came to bring me back. When I wouldn't leave my *maman* came and they did a binding spell and brought me back by force!" And oh how that had hurt. She'd begged them, pleaded to be allowed to stay and wait but they'd ganged up on her and spelled her against her will. The betrayal of that stung deep. Not as deep as it had when they'd essentially kept her prisoner with binding spells so she couldn't leave the house, and even at that moment, couldn't leave the city.

"I haven't spoken to my family, not civilly, for months. I've been at Lee's. I finally came back home two weeks ago. Even though they undid the spell to hold me bound in the house, until yesterday I was bound to stay in this fucking city!"

"Em, *a ghra*, you're angry with me for that? I didn't know!"

She stopped, just inches from him, her hands aching to touch him. She whispered, "I knew you'd come back. Everyone kept telling me that you'd dumped me. I told them you'd come back for me. They wouldn't listen to me, they wouldn't *believe* in me. They only let me come home when I lied. I said that I was healing, that I knew you weren't coming back but that I accepted it." Her voice broke. "I lied, Con. I looked into my mother's face and said I was over you. But I wasn't. I just had to be here, away from everyone. I knew that if I lied long enough that they'd believe it and I could find a way to get back to London. I think Simone knew I was lying but she didn't say anything to them. I felt my mother remove the binding spell yesterday."

He got to his knees before her and pulled her to him, his face resting against her stomach. "A thousand pardons. Please forgive me, Em." Tears choked him, the last time he'd cried was three thousand years before when his father had died. "I would never leave you."

Touching him, his scent washed over her and she allowed herself to believe that he was really there. Joy came to her then for the first time in months. "You came back," she whispered, her voice raw with anguish. "I told them all that you loved me and that you'd be back but you never came. I was afraid I'd start to believe you never would."

"I'm so sorry. I was telling my brother and sister-in-law about you, about us. I stayed the night with my mother. My mother and Magda, my brother's wife, are busily planning for our Joining ceremony right now. I would never deliberately hurt you." He looked up into her eyes, eyes that had dark circles beneath them. "I love you."

She closed her eyes and put her hands on his head. He bowed, almost in benediction to her. He shimmered them out of the apartment and into the bedroom of his flat in Paris.

"This is better, isn't it?" He stood and pulled her back to him. "Let me make it up to you."

She looked around at the apartment overlooking the Seine, taking in the expensive furnishings. The man had really good taste. "Where are we?"

He pulled her close and bent to pull her hands to his mouth to kiss them. "Our apartment in Paris." He looked down and his grin slid away as he noticed the ring was gone. "What happened to your ring?"

"*Maman* let me wear it for a month but then when they did the binding spell they removed it. Alex gave it back to me when I moved back to my apartment. They were really angry at him for doing it but he did it anyway." She pulled a chain out from under her shirt and he saw it there. "I wore it next to my heart."

"*A ghrá mo chroí*, my heart aches to think of your family believing I'd used you and abandoned you. Worse, that my absence gave them—and you—a reason to think so. Will you wear it on your finger again? Will you still join with me?"

"I never thought that. Don't you see? I may have felt despair the longer you were gone but I never gave up hope. I missed hearing your Gaelic," she said softly as she pulled the chain from her neck and handed him the ring that she unbound from it.

He took it and slid it back onto her finger. "I'm so sorry. Do you forgive me?"

"There's nothing to forgive. I knew you'd be back and you are. If you didn't know, how can I hold it against you? I took a leap of faith and you deserved it."

He kissed the hand that wore his ring and pulled her to him tightly. "My gods, Em, you're skin and bones." Shocked, he stepped back and really looked at her. In addition to the dark circles ringing her eyes her clothes hung from her body. Her normally shiny ebony hair had lost its luster. "This is because of me," he said. It wasn't a question. Guilt knifed through him.

"It's over," she said, reaching out to caress the line of his jaw. If she'd ever doubted his love, she knew the truth now. It was clear in his face, the way he watched her greedily. "You're here now. I look like crap, but you're here."

He took her hand. "Come. I'm going to take care of you. I'll run your bath and you'll eat." He led her into his bathroom and turned on the taps for the huge bathtub. "Wait," he said and clothes appeared in a neat pile on the padded seat near the vanity.

She smiled at him and felt the awful weight of her despair lift from her heart. He pulled her shirt off over her head and sucked in a breath when he saw her ribs. She'd been lean before, but more in an athletic sense. She was now much too thin. "We need to fix this," he said determinedly. "How could your family have let you get this thin?" he said angrily as he helped her into the water and then joined her after he'd summoned off his own clothes.

"Don't you attack them! They did the best they could. You forget that I'm an empath—I could feel what they all felt as this whole thing happened. You have no idea how hard it was for my mother to look me in the face and tell me that I'd been abandoned. It tore her up inside. When I wouldn't leave the penthouse they had to spell me to bind and silence me because I was screaming for you over and over.

"When I got back here I kept insisting that you were coming back but they wouldn't listen. Oh I was so angry. I haven't spoken a single unnecessary word to any of them in months. But they all continued to try and take care of me even though I wouldn't acknowledge them.

"Every day my *grandmere* would bring me some new treat to entice me to eat. They baked me all of my favorites. Once I moved back to my apartment, Lee brought me food every day. Aidan sent to Austria for the chocolates I love so much. I just gave up for a while. I was so lost without you and I didn't know how to find my way back. Even though I'm angry at them for not believing in you, for not believing in me, they still did everything they knew how to do, Con."

She was on her knees facing him, eyes sparking with her earnest defense of those she loved. He imagined that she did the same when she defended him to her family. For the first time since he'd seen her that day, he saw a glimpse of his Em—the Em that he'd left yesterday. He reached up and brushed a fingertip over her nipples.

"My apologies. Your family obviously loves you and they don't know me so how could they understand that I'd never leave you? We will have to change that. After you've eaten and I've made love to you a few times we'll go back to New Orleans so that I can meet them and we can patch this up. I don't like the idea of you not speaking to them."

She moved closer and he slid a soapy hand up her neck and pulled her to him. His lips tasted her gently and she let out a sigh, a sound of such sweet yearning that it set him afire. Struggling, he stanched his own desire and slowly soaped her body, from the sweet-smelling shampoo that he massaged into her hair all the way down to the soap he used on her toes.

He looked at her as she lay back against the rim of the tub, floating in his arms, totally relaxed. She slowly opened her eyes and locked her gaze to his. The light from the candles that he'd placed around the bathroom flickered and winked off the walls, reflecting in the mirrors. Her skin was flushed, glowing.

Reaching out to touch him, she caressed the long line of his muscular neck. "Con, I know I'm a bit skinny right now and I look like hell, but I need you," she whispered.

He sat up with an anguished cry and embraced her. He kissed the top of her head and down to her ears. "*A ghra*, you are a beauty, a stirring sight to my eyes. I want you every moment I'm awake and I dream of you each night. I need you too, I always need you."

"Then take me. Fill me up until I can't take another inch. I've been so empty inside."

He ran more clean, hot water after getting rid of the soapy water. Sitting on the carved step inside the large bathtub, he pulled her onto his lap facing him. He brought her to his mouth, ravenous for a taste of her. She sucked his bottom lip between her teeth, worrying it gently. His hands slid down her spine and cupped the curve of her bottom, fingertips brushing over her pussy and the puckered star of her anus. She made a mewl of pleasure deep in her throat and he got even harder.

When he sucked her tongue into his mouth he tasted sorrow and love, hope and trust. Their tongues slid against each other and he groaned low when her hands found his ears and she gently traced over the tips.

He slid two fingers inside her and her back arched to take him deeper. His lips left her mouth and he latched onto a nipple. She cried out with joy as that pink point of pleasure hardening under his questing tongue—the nipple elongating as her pleasure built. A thumb flicked across the swollen surface of her clit and she shuddered.

She pressed her lips to his ear, biting the lobe and nibbling the outer edge, slowly, slowly until she sucked the tip of it into her mouth and grazed her teeth over it.

"Oh yesss," he groaned.

"Do you like that? Hmmm?" she whispered breathily into his ear. "It's almost as sensitive as your cock. Shall I lick it again, Con?" she asked and then swirled her tongue over the point, gently biting it.

His back arched, fingers digging into her hips.

"Fuck me, Con. Please. I don't want the preliminaries, not now. Right now I need your big hard cock deep inside of my pussy."

The thrill of the words that she had been so shy to say not too very long before rushed through his system. She was so wet and hot, so ready for him. He lifted her and plunged her down onto his cock. She screamed and bowed her back, knees tight at his hips.

"Oh god, yes, like that!" she exclaimed. The way he filled her made her feel complete for the first time in months.

"Ride me then, Em, my sweet," he growled, his lips around a nipple.

She slowly rose up, pulling herself almost completely off his cock and then slid down ever so slowly, milking every bit of pleasure out of the moment that she could. "That's so good, Con."

"Mmmm," was all he could manage to say as she took him back into her body again.

The water gently rolled against them as she moved, almost like caressing fingers. Given the depth of the water in the huge tub she felt partially weightless and it gave her a delicious buoyancy.

She wanted to pull him deep inside her. Not just his cock but all of him. After so much time without him, his physical presence was like a healing balm. Something about him called out to her, made her restlessness disappear, made her whole. Everything that had been wrong and felt out of place suddenly shifted and fit back together again.

Con reached for a bottle of oil, pulled out the stopper and poured it over her upper body. He began to massage it into her skin with his large hands, taking extra care with her nipples as he tugged and rolled them between his fingers.

The oil made the water slick and the friction suddenly turned slippery.

"It's a special oil, edible, an excellent lubricant too. Your skin feels so incredibly soft," he murmured as his hands smoothed the slick oil across her skin, massaging her aches and warming her.

She sped up on him, needing to feel him stronger, harder. She yanked on his hair to angle his head where she needed it to be for her kisses and her hands went to his ears.

His cock sliced through her wet heat over and over as the inferno in her core continued to simmer, sending scalding waves of pleasure down her spine, up from her toes.

He began to thrust then, holding her down on him while he pressed up into her. "So fucking tight and hot," he grunted as he slammed into her over and over.

Her head lolled back and she stiffened and came with a long scream when he slid a finger into her rear passage and stroked.

Her pussy clamped down on him like a vise, milking him with her climax. "I want you to come inside of me," she whispered into his ear. Her words drove him hard and he continued to piston into her as she kept her fingers on his ears. He was seeing pinpoints of light and his teeth began to tingle. He thrust up hard, lifting her body up as his own arched up to meet hers. His cum shot out of his body and bathed her womb over and over again until he had nothing left but the pounding of his heart.

After several minutes of laying there with her in his arms, he stood her up and rinsed her body of soap, sweat and seed and helped her out. He slowly buffed her dry with a big fluffy towel and held out a silky robe for her to slip into.

She looked up into his face, sliding a hand along his jaw and up and over his ear. "Thank you." She felt so cherished then, cared for and loved. His hands were almost reverent.

He kissed her roughly in his eagerness to show her how much he loved her. "Don't thank me, Em. You know that your pleasure is my job," he growled at her. "Now, we're getting lunch and you're going to eat two helpings."

He made her eat a sizeable luncheon, feeding her from his own plate when she finished with hers. Each bite she took made him feel better, as if she were taking a big step back toward him.

"I suppose we need to deal with your family. I can't imagine that they're very happy with me right now," he said as he watched her chest rise and fall with her breathing, each intake of breath giving him the barest glimpse of her areola.

"Well, about that... Why don't I talk with them first before you show up?"

"Because from now on we do this together. I don't want to leave you alone to face them. I want them to see that I'll stand up with you even when things are rough. Before we go, though, I spoke to the queen and she has agreed to bring you over, to grant you immortality. I'd take you over right now to do it but I don't want so much time to move by here while we are there. I don't want your family to worry about you any more than they already have."

"What is the ratio of time passage from there to here anyway? Can't we just factor that in?"

"No, it's not that simple. Time moves differently there but not just in comparison to here. Sometimes I can sift between worlds and just a few minutes or hours have passed. Other instances, like this time, months can pass by. One never knows. When I'm here on assignment like I was with you, I would only sift there and back for a few minutes." He shrugged. "Just to be sure that I'd come back quickly. Although, and I swear this to you, I had no idea that so much time would pass. I never would have stayed that long if I had known."

"Stop beating yourself up over it. My family will have to accept all of this after I explain. Say, what's the difference between sifting and shimmering? Or are they the same? Sometimes you call it sifting, sometimes you call it shimmering."

"When one travels between worlds, like between here and Tir na nOg, it's sifting—you're sifting between dimensions. Traveling from one point to another on the same world or dimension is shimmering. As in, when you and I go to New Orleans to deal with your family, we'll be shimmering," he said, getting back to the subject.

"Are you sure you don't want me to go in first? It's liable to be pretty bad at first."

"*A ghra*, we're going to be together forever. They'll have to get used to me sometime. Plus, well, I don't mean to brag but I do seem to do pretty well with the ladies," he said teasingly but saw the flash of hurt in her eyes. He touched her cheek. "*Mo fiach*, why do you do that to yourself? How can you doubt me? Even now?"

"I'm working on it, I really am. I've had a lot of time to think, to work through things over the last three months. But you haven't met my sister or my mother. I just...well, I've never been as powerful as the other women in my family. Or as exciting, or as beautiful or sexy," she added quietly, her eyes locked to his. That was an improvement. Months ago she would have looked down or away from him.

"Em, you are everything to me. Do you not understand this yet? Can you not see your own beauty and intelligence?

Your own powers of intuition and empathy? The first time I saw you, you went straight to my heart and you've dug into my system every moment since. While I am sure the other women in your family are all beautiful and strong, they cannot hold a candle to you. Subject closed," he said with such arrogance that she gave up and kissed his nose with a grin.

He looked at her and he was wearing jeans and a light sweater and then they both were standing in her living room.

"Jeez! Warn a girl before you do that, will you?" she exclaimed with surprise.

He shrugged as looked around, nose wrinkled in distaste. "This place is a mess."

"Yeah, well, my life was a mess."

He put her hand over his heart and then brought it to his lips. "My apologies. Shall we go to deal with your family now?"

"May as well. But let's take the human way, all right? We can meet at Lee's house. It's more neutral than my parents' place." She picked up the phone and made calls, arranging to meet in an hour at her sister's home.

She looked at him. "It'll just be my immediate family tonight, and Aidan and Alex. If we get through this alive the news will trickle outward to everyone else." She went into her bedroom and rifled through the closet. "I really need to do laundry," she muttered.

"Let me help," Con said and suddenly the silky robe was replaced by a pair of cool linen pants and a sleeveless shirt. He'd even conjured a lovely pair of kate spade kitten heels to go with it.

"Perfect. This outfit is perfect. How do you do it?"

"I saw you looking at it in London," he said with a shrug. "Now, we need to talk about other details. Where we'll live when we are here in New Orleans and when we'll go to Tir na nOg to do the Joining and for the queen to transform you." He looked around the apartment with disdain.

"Listen, buster, this place isn't so bad!"

"Em, this place is small, dark and cramped. I took the liberty of looking into buying something." He shimmered them into the foyer of a large home. "This place is lovely, is it not?"

She walked through the foyer and into the house. The rooms were spacious and filled with antiques. She stood in the doorway of a gigantic library, complete with reading nook in an open second floor loft. Books lined every wall from floor to ceiling.

"These are my magic texts. When did you do this?"

"Yes. They'd need to be wherever you are of course so I moved them just now. Nice magic trick, hmm? The rest of this I did while you were running around the world trying to track the book down."

She looked back at him and shook her head in wonder. They climbed a beautifully carved grand staircase. She went into the master suite and gasped. There were French doors leading out to a terrace that overlooked the river. "This is a plantation house!"

"Yes, or so the paperwork said. I'm guessing this is a good thing?"

Incredulous, she continued to stare at him for a moment and then looked back out over the grounds. "It's breathtaking. How can you afford such a thing? I most certainly can't."

"Em, money means nothing to the Fae. It's easy to conjure, just like your clothes. When I was watching you, you came out to one of these houses, back in March, with a visiting cousin. You seemed so smitten with it I thought you might like to live in one. I wanted the one you visited but they wouldn't sell it."

"Oak Alley? Only one of the most famous historical homes in the state? Yeah, I don't suppose they would," she said with a laugh and then reached out and snuggled into his body. "Thank you, Con."

He smiled, absurdly happy that such a small thing could make her so pleased. "We'll begin to live here tonight then."

"Tonight?"

"Yes, why not? The furniture is here, the refrigerator and pantry are stocked. It's your house, why shouldn't you live in it?"

"Is everything so easily solved with you?"

"No, not everything. But, Em, I want to make you happy. I want you to be comfortable and surrounded by luxury. That's easy for me and it pleases me to see you pleased." He shrugged and kissed the top of her head. "I love you."

Her bottom lip trembled. "I love you, too."

He shimmered them back to her apartment. "Now, when shall we go back to Tir na nOg?"

"Tomorrow? I need to talk to my family and explain things and then we can go and meet yours."

"And you're sure you wish to be immortal? To be converted into what I am?"

"Are you sure you want me to be?" she countered.

"I love you, get that through your adorably thick head! It isn't something my queen takes lightly. Humans have only been converted less than a hundred times over the tens upon tens of thousands of years she's existed. I have served her for nearly ten thousand years. She has granted my request because she can see how much I love you."

"Then yes, I want to be converted into what you are. I'm going to have to get used to the time thing, I can't be gone from my family for years at a time. If I'm going to be immortal, I have to spend the time I can with them. I need to cherish their mortality." A hint of sadness marked her eyes.

She was so kind and loving. He pulled her into his arms and kissed her temple. "We will work it out the best we can. Of course you want to be here with your family as much as you can be. You'll be able to shimmer and sift at will when you become Fae, you know. We'll spend lots of time in your New Orleans, I promise."

Her smile brightened and she nodded.

A corner of his mouth quirked up. He flicked a hand and her apartment was straightened up. Another flick and her closet and drawers were empty, the walls next, then the bookshelves and counters.

"All moved in. Shall we go to your sister's house now?"

She laughed and they walked out to her car.

* * * * *

Lee put the phone back in the cradle and looked at Alex and Aidan. "That was Em. He's back. She wants to meet here in an hour."

Alex smiled. He knew that Em wouldn't have trusted the Fae without good reason. He looked at Aidan, who returned the same smile. They had both argued with Lee and the rest of the Charvezes that Em should be trusted but to no avail.

"I won't say I told you so," Aidan said smoothly, using his sensual thrall of voice to send sex with his words. Alex's cock hardened at the sound and seeing it, Aidan gave a wicked grin as he reached out to stroke it. They both watched as Lee's annoyance faded into something else.

"We don't have time for this," she said softly, eyes glued to Aidan's hand popping open the buttons on the fly of Alex's jeans.

"Ah, darlin', we always have time for an appetizer," Aidan said as Alex popped out into his hand.

"Five minutes! I have to call my mother. Don't you dare start without me!" She turned and quickly dialed the phone as Aidan met Alex's lips with his own.

* * * * *

Con vowed that if he survived Em's driving he'd never allow her behind the wheel again. His hands were sore from the death grip he'd kept on the door as she careened through the streets of New Orleans, once narrowly missing a collision with a streetcar. "My gods! Are you trying to kill me? You drive like a berserker," he shouted as she pulled up in front of Lee's.

She rolled her eyes as he took her car keys from her hands. "You're immortal. Big baby." And he laughed as she stuck her tongue out at him.

They walked through the gate and he sucked in a breath. "I'm impressed. The level of warding is very complicated. Your sister did this?"

"No, although she probably could. She's capable of just about anything."

There was admiration there in her voice, admiration and deep affection. He put his arm around her shoulder and the door yanked open and a tiny redhead stood there, fury on her face.

"Get your hands off her! You bastard, how dare you show your face back here after you abandoned her in London!" she shouted.

Before Con could say anything Em stood between him and her sister and glared. "That's enough, Lee. We've come to explain but if you can't be civil, I'll leave right now."

Con squeezed the arm around her shoulder to calm her. "*A ghra*, don't get so upset."

"Con, I appreciate your concern but this is between Lee and me." She looked back to her sister and Con saw Aidan Bell standing there with a shorter, muscular man he assumed was the wizard that Em had spoken so fondly of.

"Lee, please," Aidan said as he put a hand on her shoulder and smiled at Em. "Hey, sweet, it's good to see you looking happy again," he said and Con felt a bit better knowing that his old friend cared for Em's happiness so much.

"Aidan, thank you," Em said and looked back to her sister. "Are you going to invite us in or do I need to leave?"

Lee sighed and stepped back, waving them inside. Con could feel the menace coming from her as he followed Em into a front parlor, where he joined her on a couch.

Several other people came in and suddenly it was auditory chaos. There was screeching and yelling and cursing. A tall, dark-haired woman and an older man with reddish hair were there and two other men, probably in their late twenties or early thirties, had joined the fray.

Em stood up and stuck her fingers into her mouth and whistled loud and long. The din quieted and they all stared at her, surprised.

"Let me explain for god's sake! No one talks until I'm done. Please."

"You let this pig touch you again? After what he did to you? Do you so suddenly have amnesia? He caused you to shut your family out for months! You lost so much weight that I thought we'd have to put you in the hospital!" an older woman exclaimed.

Con jerked and looked at Em, who was blushing. "Hospital?"

"I said, no one talks until I'm done!" Em said, voice getting louder with each word.

"Let's let Em talk, shall we?" Alex said.

Everyone sank into a chair or a couch and grudgingly shut up, waiting.

Em took a deep breath and told them all the story of the differing time lines and of how Con had come back to her only a day after he'd left her, totally unaware that months had passed.

"He did not know. I told you he'd never abandon me but you all found it so easy to believe that a man like Con could never love a woman like me. You never believed in me." Her voice broke then and Con, while not an empath, could feel the waves of sorrow roll from her. He closed his eyes for a moment and took a deep breath, waiting for her to continue. He put his arm around her shoulders and pulled her to him.

"How can you think that?" Lee asked. "The way we felt was not about you, it was about him. Of course you could be loved. Any man would be lucky to have a woman like you, Em. Where did this idea that we don't believe in you come from?"

"I told you that he didn't abandon me! You wouldn't believe me. You took away my free will with that binding spell! You kept me here against my wishes. I am an adult and you—*all* of you—treated me like a child. You didn't listen to me and you bound me to a place I didn't want to be."

Con thought of the fierce way she'd defended her family to him earlier. She was so cornered she had nowhere to go. She loved them all so much but they'd hurt her, even as she herself was hurt by his attack on them.

"Look at what this creep has done to you, Em. You were a nice quiet girl, shy and sweet, and you meet this jerk and suddenly you won't listen to your family, we have to drag you back here kicking and screaming! How do you know he wasn't off with someone else for the last three months? All you've got is his word, the word of a guy who ditched you for *three* months, Em. You deserve better than this." The tall man looked at Em with pleading eyes.

"Niall, are you saying that because I believed that Con loved me I am not nice anymore? And once and for all—I am not the shy, sweet girl you all think I am! That's who you all *wanted* me to be and you've just kept pigeonholing me that way. I work with books. That doesn't make me shy!"

Niall looked at Em and snorted. "See what I mean? You've never exploded this way at your family before. You chose an outsider over us. He's turned you against us."

The older woman who was clearly their mother turned and looked sharply at the man who'd spoken, but Con stood up before she could say anything. "Are you deliberately trying to hurt your own sister? Do you think she's so stupid and weak that she'd believe a lie like that? And do you not trust her beauty and intelligence to attract someone better than a man who'd only lie to her?" Con's hands were clenched. He wanted to pull Em to him and protect her from this but he knew she'd resent him if he did.

"The Conchobar MacNessa that I know is an honorable man. As I've said before, although I've never been through the Veil to Tir na nOg, if he says that time passes differently, I'd believe it. The two worlds are very different. If I recall correctly the same laws of physics do not apply," Aidan said quietly.

"Tir na nOg is basically a construct of the magic and imagination of the Sidhe. When we fought our last wars and lost, we sought refuge there. Will and imagination are in the air. The Fae are older than you can imagine. Time, at least in the sense that humans perceive it, is more or less meaningless to beings who are tens of thousands of years old," Con explained and the older woman nodded.

"You don't know what we went though, watching her fall apart. Watching her lose it bit by bit, pulling away from us more each day until we had no choice but to keep her bound to stay first in the house and then in the city," the other young man, clearly Lee's twin, spoke. "She seems to have some crazy idea that we don't believe in her but I know she felt what we did when we had to hold her down while *Maman* and Lee prepared the binding spell. While they had to force-feed her and we considered putting her in the hospital to get her a feeding IV because she'd gotten so thin. How we felt watching our sweet Em who each day continued to waste away into a shadow. You did that."

Em winced and Con's heart paused a moment.

"Let's do some introductions, shall we?" Aidan interrupted. He pointed to the older woman and the man beside her. "Emile Brousard and Marie Charvez, Em's *maman* and *papa*."

Con inclined his head.

Aidan turned to the belligerent man. "That is Niall, Em's oldest brother and next to him is Eric, her next oldest sibling and Lee's fraternal twin. The gorgeous redhead here is Lee and the man beside her is Alex, Lee's other husband. All of you, this is Conchobar MacNessa."

Con took a deep breath and Em took his hand and kissed it. That small gesture helped him regain his composure and his intention to clear the air and make peace with these people who were so very important to Em.

"Niall, you are right. I did that. I hurt Em and I take full responsibility for it but I tell you truly, I did not know. I would never, ever, hurt her on purpose. I love her. I have been alive ten millennia. I have never, in all of that time, fallen in love. You have no idea how special she is to me and so I cannot blame you for being angry with me for hurting your sister and daughter the way I did. But she and I have moved past it. She's forgiven me and I hope that you can too."

Em took a deep breath. "There was nothing to forgive. He didn't know. He didn't intend to hurt me or to be gone for so long. I expect all of you to understand this salient point." She squeezed his hand and moved on quickly. "And...I am going to Tir na nOg tomorrow with Con. We are going to have a Joining ceremony and I'm going to be made into an immortal."

"What!" her father exploded and jumped to his feet. "This is insanity. First Niall is gay, then Lee marries a vampire and then marries *another* man who's a wizard. Now Em is going to some place where she could be gone from here for years or decades and she's going to turn into a Faerie too? Enough is enough! I blame you, Marie, for being so damned permissive with them all. I forbid it, Emily Charvez. You'll do no such thing." He sat back down, arms crossed over his chest.

Em looked at Lee and then at her mother. They all stayed silent for a moment and then began to laugh. The men watched, amused. Em was laughing so hard that tears were running down her face. She gasped for breath. "Well, thank god Eric is normal, huh, *Papa*?"

Which started another round of laughter. Emile just looked at them, shaking his head. "Make fun, go ahead. Don't come to me, Marie, when Em is off in Never Neverland with Peter Pan over there."

"Peter Pan wasn't a Faerie," Niall said.

"But you are!" Lee said, between guffaws.

"Hardy har har. Heck, you're the one in the threesome! I may be gay but I'm only sleeping with one guy," Niall said with a grin.

Con watched them all in disbelief but also relief as he saw the ties that bound them all together slowly start to weave themselves back together again. He met Aidan's eyes and the other man nodded with a small smile.

"Really, I blame Eric for being normal," Em said, face serious.

"I'll bet he wears Delia's clothes when she isn't home," Marie said.

"*Maman!*" Eric exclaimed with a grin. "You're all crazy." He looked at Con. "You sure you want her now? We all come with the bargain. We're nosy and infuriating and constantly giving unwanted advice."

Con smiled then. "Wait until you meet my family."

* * * * *

The two women alone in the living room, Lee handed Em a glass of wine and sat next to her on the couch, tucking her feet beneath her. "You want to tell me what's been making you so unhappy this last year?"

Con and Alex and Aidan were all in the study, drinking cognac and talking. Everyone else had gone home after they'd talked for another hour about their plans for the immediate future. For the time being at least, things were okay.

Em took a sip of the ruby red liquid and reached out and tugged on a long, coppery spiral of her sister's hair. "I've been the less talented, less beautiful little sister to Lee Charvez my whole life. Niall and Eric have brilliant legal careers, *Maman* is a witch dreamer, you're not only a witch dreamer but the most powerful witch in generations. Hell, you ran off to Tulane and *Maman* still put the majority of her attention on you. You weren't even around and I was still in your shadow.

"I just began to feel like I couldn't get out from under it all. Like I was no one except in relation to you or some other powerful female in our family. Worse, you all have this idea of me in your heads — Em the shy one, Em the quiet one. That isn't who I am! You have no idea what it's like to have your identity constantly be shaped by the way other people perceive you."

Lee wove her fingers through her sister's. "How can you not see yourself? How powerful you are, how beautiful and intelligent? I may be more powerful as a witch, but what you know about magic, about history and the arcane arts, is beyond anyone I know. You're one of the world's foremost magical scholars and you're twenty-five years old. People come to you from far and wide to seek your knowledge, your expertise.

"More than that, you're the most intuitive person I've ever met. It's more than just being a feeler, Em. More than being empathic, you're a lot like a seeress. It's amazing and it never ceases to blow me away."

Lee looked lovingly at her sister's gamine features. The big green eyes, the tousled onyx hair, the regal cheekbones. "Beauty-wise, how can you not feel how men see you? Don't tell me that you are never desired because that's plain impossible."

"Yes, men look at my body and feel desire. At the same time, I'm too tall for many of them, or worse, they see you and wonder why I can't be more like you. Why I'm not a petite little doll with delicate features." Em shrugged. "But I don't feel so miserable anymore. I believed in myself, Lee. I believed that Con wouldn't leave me and he didn't. I took a leap of faith, the biggest in my life and after everything, I believed in myself and I won.

"Each day I woke up and he hadn't returned but I kept faith. Faith in myself and faith in him. The days passed into weeks and then months. You all kept telling me that he'd abandoned me and I admit that it got harder to keep believing. Sometimes I had to give up for a while, turn off thinking because I couldn't bear to let go of my belief in Con but I also had a hard time reconciling reality with what I knew to be true. I couldn't afford to let myself doubt.

"But today before he showed up, I was drinking a cup of tea and I realized that even if he had abandoned me that I'd be okay. That my heart would be broken and a part of me would be missing but that I would get past it someday.

"I found myself because of him. No, not like I needed a man to make my life as a woman worthwhile or anything. But by letting myself take a leap of faith, believing in myself either way, I shook off that shadow."

Lee leaned in and kissed her sister's cheek. "I'm sorry I didn't believe that he was coming back. I swear to you that it wasn't because I didn't think you were worthy of being loved by Con. I thought he wasn't worthy of you. I thought you'd been taken in by him. I'm sorry I took away your will. I thought I was doing what was best for you. I love you, Emmy."

Em hugged her tightly. "I know. I never doubted that. Yes, I was angry and hurt, but I always knew that everything you all did was from love."

"I saw the way he looks at you. He loves you, Em. He adores you. I'm glad you found that. That depth of love from the person your heart is meant to love, it's the best thing that ever happened to me and now you have it too."

"And I'll have a long lifespan too. I'll miss everyone but at least you'll still be around."

Lee nodded. "Not for ten thousand years but for a good long time. Most of the time, I try not to think about losing everyone. I must admit that I feel better knowing you'll be with me."

Con came into the room. "*Mo fiach*, you must be tired. Shall we go?"

"You need the sleep. You'll come back soon?" Lee asked as she hugged her sister.

"Yes. But it could be months. Remember that the time moves differently there. I may be gone for longer than you expect but know that I'll be back. I'll always be back. We have our house to come back to. You all to come back to. And *Maman* will kill me if we don't let her plan a wedding of some sort soon." She looked at her sister standing there with Alex and Aidan. "I love you."

They all hugged her. "We love you, too. Con, take care of her or I'll have to kick your ass," Alex said.

Con nodded and they shimmered home.

* * * * *

Once they were back at their new house, Con stared down at her, fury on his face. "Why did you not tell me about the hospital? You were so thin they thought you needed to be put on a feeding tube! You are not allowed to put your health in danger like that, Em. I forbid it!"

"What good would it have done to have told you about all sorts of might-have-beens? You weren't here, Con! When you came back, it wasn't your fault you were gone so long and if I'd told you it only would have hurt you. I didn't want to make you feel any worse. Anyway, I have been eating!"

He tipped her chin up with a finger and kissed her softly. "*Is tusa mo shaol*, you are my world, don't you know that? Do you know what it felt like to hear about how truly precarious your health was from your mother and brother? Yes, it would have made me feel worse but it made me feel pretty bad to have heard it from someone other than you."

"I'm sorry."

They walked upstairs to the master suite and he slowly peeled her clothes off. He tucked her in the large bed and got in beside her.

"Eat," he said, and he created a tray of fruit and cheese that he shoved at her. "And then tell me about it. All of it and don't apologize."

She shrugged and looked at him as she ate. "I wouldn't accept that you weren't coming back. I was angry at them for not letting me go back to London. It got...bad. I wasn't speaking to them, but they're my main emotional support. I just sort of pulled into myself. I lost the weight and they got so very worried about me and threatened to hospitalize me on the advice of our doctor if I didn't get my act together. I finally agreed to eat and get back on track but only if they let me leave and come back to my apartment."

He kissed her gently. "I am sorry for these last three months, sorry that you nearly lost yourself because of me."

"Don't you see, Con? I found myself because of you. I made it through and I know that I can. Today I stood up to my family in a way I never would have before, Niall was right about that. I stood up for myself and made them hear me. Things will be better now that I've said things that needed to be said to them."

"Oh, my sweet Em," he whispered as he fed her a strawberry and lapped up the juice that rimmed her lips.

Chapter Eleven

ഇ

Em woke to the sound of the ocean and the smell of flowers. She slowly opened her eyes and started. She sat up and looked around the room she was in. She lay on a large bed facing a wall, or rather a large opening leading to the sea. But it was like no sea she'd ever seen—the water was a brilliant teal blue and glittered like a gemstone. The sand was a pale blond-white and looked smooth and soft. It certainly wasn't Louisiana.

She looked around but Con wasn't anywhere to be seen. Getting up, she padded naked across the cool, tiled floor and into the next room where she heard movement and smelled coffee. Smiling, she saw Con leaning against a wall, one foot crossed over the other, drinking from a mug. He looked beautiful and relaxed. He was wearing soft gray pants with a drawstring waist and a shirt that he hadn't bothered to button. She wanted to gobble him up.

Smiling, she walked toward him and put her arms around his neck. "Morning. Mind telling me where the heck we are?"

He looked startled and spun her quickly, putting her back against the wall where he'd been leaning, his body shielding hers. "Jaysus, Em!" He pulled off his shirt and put it onto her body while she protested and squirmed.

"What?"

"You must be Em. Con has told me all about you. Well, clearly not all."

Face burning with embarrassment, she peeked around Con's body to see a tall man with flame red hair and the same braids that Con wore at the temples standing there with a devilish smile on his face.

She smacked Con on the arm in embarrassment. "Hello! It would be nice to know what the hell is going on here."

"You're the one who is naked in front of company," he said, trying not to smile.

"Where the heck are we?"

"Welcome to Tir na nOg, Em. This is our home and the man behind me—who will be missing some teeth if he doesn't stop trying to see your body—is, or rather used to be, my best friend Jayce MacTavish."

"It would have been nice for you to have told me you were going to blink us here so I wouldn't walk out naked in front of guests," she hissed and without being able to help herself, kissed his bare chest, over his heart.

"I wanted you to wake up smelling the sea and the flowers, I wanted you to know why Tir na nOg is so special," he said softly, kissing the top of her head, breathing her in.

She softened. "You're damned good, MacNessa. I'll bet that line got you loads of ass over the millennia."

Jayce threw back his head and laughed and she ducked her head around Con again. "It's nice to meet you, sorry to flash you. I'll be out in a few minutes," she called and scampered into the bedroom, which unlike the open wall that faced the sea had an actual door.

She puttered around, finding her clothes in a large closet. Well, she supposed they were hers. Con had clearly been up to his magical shopping spree again because the clothes hanging up were all new. She could see Con's stamp all over them, especially when she opened the drawers of the built-in dressers and saw all the sexy underthings.

She took a long shower in his gargantuan shower enclosure that was open to the sky and got dressed in a simple blouse and soft, silky skirt that came to mid-thigh.

"Much better," she said as she came out into the living area and handed Con his shirt back.

"For you maybe. I much preferred what you weren't wearing before," Jayce joked and she laughed too while Con scowled.

"Don't you have somewhere to be, Jayce?"

"The whole place is all atwitter over the human who stole your heart. I'm surprised that I'm the only guest this morning."

Jayce had warned Con that there were a few people, mainly females, who were mightily unhappy about his plans to join with a human woman. Mainly though, people were just curious about the whole thing. A slightly troubling development was that the contingent of Dark Fae were agitated that a human was being brought into their ranks. The Dark ones hated humans and the main reason they'd been on the outs with the rest of the Fae in the last four thousand years was because the Fae felt it was their duty to protect and interfere as little as possible with humanity. But the Dark Fae thought that humans were there for the enslavement and amusement of the Fae because they were an advanced race.

"Are people upset?" Em asked, alarmed.

Con put his arm around her and handed her a cup. She sniffed it. "Coffee? You drink coffee in faerieland?"

Jayce laughed again.

"You can drink whatever you want to here. And don't let anyone else hear you call it that until they get to know you," Con said, pushing her to sit at the table and putting a plate filled with food before her. "Now eat, you're too skinny."

"Words every girl wants to hear," she said and began to eat, watching Con and Jayce. "And I'm human but not an idiot. I'm not going to go and alienate people."

"How do you know you didn't alienate Jayce?" Con asked smugly.

She sighed. "Conchobar MacNessa, have you forgotten what I am? I'm a feeler, I detected quite a few things from

Jayce." She winked at him and he chuckled. "None of them was anger or alienation."

Con gave his friend a dirty look and then looked back to Em. "I thought you couldn't feel Fae?"

"I can't feel you. Apparently it sometimes it works that way with empaths and people they're very close to. My *grandmere* told me that most of us have ended up with partners that we've been unable to read. It was another reason I believed you were coming back. Sometimes it's because of the other person's power level—I can't read Lee—and other times it's due to familial ties, which is also part of why I can't read Lee. I can read Jayce loud and clear," she said and hastily added, "but, Jayce, I do turn it down as far as I can when I'm with friends and out in public. I don't snoop. It just comes from people."

He put his hand on hers and smiled. "I'm not worried, Em. I thank you, though, for your reassurance."

"Get your paws off my wife," Con growled and Jayce laughed again.

"So what do you do, Jayce?"

"I'm one of the Queen's Favored, as Con is."

Con had explained that the Queen's Favored was a council of advisors and warriors, sort of like a presidential cabinet. Con sat at Aine's right hand, her most trusted advisor and councilor.

"When do we meet her, Con?" Em asked as she looked him over. Damn if he wasn't the sexiest thing she'd ever seen.

"As soon as you eat, *a ghra*. We'll go and wait for an audience. She'll administer the spell and you'll be one of us. Then we'll go and see my family."

She must have shown her distress because he picked her hand up and kissed it. "They'll love you, least of all because I love you. But they are all going to see what a special woman you are right away."

She turned to Jayce. "But not everyone is going to love me, isn't that true?"

"Damn, it's a good thing you love her so much, Con. She sees right through any attempts to get around her. I've got to go," he said, standing up and giving her a small bow. "I will see you at the queen's chambers. Em, it was a pleasure to meet you and see you naked. If you need any help working with your new powers, please call on me. Con was always bad at controlling the elements."

She blinked in surprise. "Oh, okay. Nice to meet you too, I'll see you later."

He shimmered out of the room before Con could toss a plate at his head.

She turned to him. "I think you've got some explaining to do, Con."

"Well, Aine isn't just going to make you immortal. You'll be Fae, with all of the things that come with it. Each of us, much like each Charvez woman, has certain gifts although we all have the same basic powers, sifting between the worlds is one. And…"

"Yeah, that's all great and I want to hear more about any cool new superpowers and all, but let's get to the part about not everyone being happy about me."

Damn, she was good. "There are some Fae who don't like humans," he said simply. "My Joining with you will agitate them."

She arched a brow. "Why would they care?"

He sighed and her eyes narrowed. "I come from kings of old. My mother is forty thousand years old and the daughter of one of the oldest of us all. My grandfather was one of the first Sidhe. He doesn't get out much, the oldest ones tend to avoid most people. He lives in a place that sits between worlds."

"So these people won't like the human marrying their golden boy?"

"Something like that. Other royal families have been trying to get our bloodlines mixed with theirs for a very long time. Finn, my brother, married a woman who is in Faerie culture considered a commoner. My mother was not pleased, although she and Magda get along quite well now."

"Oh, so she's got to be all kinds of pleased that you're bringing home a human commoner, huh?"

"She gave me her blessing once she looked into my heart and saw you there." He took her hand and put it over his heart. "She truly did. Finn and Magda as well. All of the people who truly count to me are happy for us. We can deal with the others. I just want you to be on your guard. I wish you couldn't feel them all—you're bound to feel a lot of hostility and I don't want that for you." He decided not to mention that he'd had Jayce put protective spells on her clothing as well as providing an extra set of protective eyes at the Court. While Em was human, she was incredibly vulnerable to any Fae who wished to harm her. The sooner Aine changed her the better because she'd be a lot safer. It was very difficult for him to expose her to the Court at all, thoughts of failing his father came back to haunt him. He forced himself to stop thinking about it. He'd not make the mistake of turning his attention from her for a moment.

She softened, her anger at him for neglecting to tell her that he was some kind of Faerie Kennedy had passed when she saw the concern in his face.

Sighing, she leaned into him. "It's okay, I've got you. We'll deal with the rest."

They ate and got dressed and just before he shimmered them to the queen's audience he turned to her. "Em, I hesitate to mention this but because you can feel us, there are…"

"Your former lovers will be pissed off too and present in this audience with the queen?" she finished for him, eyebrow raised.

156

He nodded. "I love you, but there are lots of women in my past, Em. I can't change that. I don't want you to feel hurt about that, what's past is past. You're my present and my eternity."

She took a deep breath. "I know. I may not have totally understood that before but I do now."

He squeezed her hand and shimmered them into Aine's audience chambers.

* * * * *

Em blinked at the brilliance of the room. Not just of the physical space—the high arches, the gleaming marble and trickle of water from fountains, the plush couches and chairs, and the drapes that looked like they had spun gold thread in them—but the people too.

The men were all large and gorgeous like Con, although not a single one could come close to how sexy Con was. The women were beautiful, their voices musical and sexy. The sound stroked over her, into her ears like a seductive caress. It was almost hypnotic. She swallowed down her feelings of inadequacy and tapped into the courage she'd found within herself. Con brought her hand to his lips and looked into her eyes. "I love you, Em," he said with a wicked grin and she smiled back, unable not to.

She opened herself up a bit as she looked around the room and felt a wide array of things—anger, fear, jealousy, resentment, curiosity, sexual attraction—both toward herself and Con. There were definitely some friendly people in the room. She felt warmth and openness and that made her relax through the feelings of definite dislike and jealousy. There was something darker there but she couldn't quite put her finger on it.

"Con, is this your little human friend?" a petite blonde said tartly as she approached and touched his arm.

Con gave a heavy sigh and squeezed Em's hand. "Sorcha, this is my Fated One, Em. Em, this is Sorcha."

"An old friend," Sorcha said with a slight leer.

"Ah, well, we all have old friends. I'm his new friend."

Em watched Sorcha's face change as the sickly sweet demeanor gave way to fury. "Look, human, I was fucking him before your kind crawled from the primordial seas."

Con started to say something but Em stepped close to the other woman. "Look, bitch, I don't care. He's with me now and that's the way it is. Deal with it or don't, it's all the same to me. As for you fucking him when the human species was nothing more than amoebae, I can't imagine why that should impress me."

She heard clapping and a musical laugh. "Well done! Sorcha, begone. I do believe you were told to be on your best behavior. Out of my sight before I remember that I used to be a goddess of vengeance."

Everyone bowed to the woman that Em guessed was the queen. She followed suit.

"Do stand and come through to my personal chambers," she called to them as she fluttered out of the room.

They followed in her wake, Con wearing a big smile. He liked this side of Em—she had taken on Sorcha like a raging lioness and the news would spread like wildfire. She'd gain respect for that. As for those who wouldn't like her for it, they didn't like her to begin with so it wasn't like she'd created new enemies.

Aine turned to them and waved at a chaise. "Sit, sit, don't bow and scrape."

Em sat tentatively and Con put his arm about the back of the chaise, keeping her close.

"Sorcha is such a bitch isn't she?" Aine laughed. "You handled it well, Em. You know you'll have several such interludes. Con was popular before he met you."

Con stiffened and started to say something but Em waved him quiet. "Please, Con, you can't be indignant over the truth. I can feel everyone but you—I can feel the story. They lust after you, yes, but mainly, they respect you. Some fear you, a few hate you, but even the ones who hate you respect your abilities."

Aine watched the human woman and her heart expanded. She could see straight into Conchobar MacNessa and see how much Em had healed his self-imposed emptiness after his father's murder. Em's love, or rather loving Em, made him stronger. Yes, Em Charvez would make an excellent Faerie as well as an excellent partner for Aine's most trusted advisor.

"You're an empath, yes?"

Em nodded. "I can't feel you, though, you've got an awful lot of power. It's blinding."

Aine smiled. Em was so genuine, there wasn't anything manipulative about the statement. It was refreshing to not have to be on her guard and wonder what the other person wanted from her. "Why thank you! I'm awfully jaded these days. I don't think I've been truly flattered or surprised or even impressed for at least forty thousand years. It will be a pleasure to have you around, Em."

With a flick of her wrist, two drinks appeared within reach of Con and Em and she took a sip of her own glass of berry wine.

Em sipped and it was so delicious she drank the whole glass in a few gulps. "That was lovely! Con, we need some of that at home," she said, delighted.

"Welcome to the Tuatha De Danann, Em," Aine said and Em felt her insides explode into bright light. Her back bowed and she would have fallen to the floor had Con not caught her and brought her to his body. He stroked a hand over her hair, murmuring in Gaelic until she came back to herself moments later.

She looked around the room and everything was brighter, sharper, more vivid and colorful. She could see the life emanating from the plants, from the water. Aine's aura was even more blinding and Con was more beautiful than he'd been through human eyes.

"Did you change her?" Con asked, worried.

"I did. How do you feel, Em?" Aine asked amused and very touched by the way Con was so concerned.

"Fantastic, Your Majesty," Em answered, continuing to be amazed.

"Please, call me Aine. You have Freya's mark, would you like to meet her?"

"The goddess...angel...whatever that made the Compact?"

"Yes."

"Sure!"

Aine crossed to her but Con put himself between them. She raised a brow. "Do you think I would make her immortal and then harm her?"

He moved back. "I beg your forgiveness, Majesty."

"As you should, Conchobar. In any case, it's sweet of you. I'll bring her to Finn's when I'm done." Aine took Em's outstretched hand and they sifted.

This time, Em felt the mechanics of the sift and understood it. The magic of it was like a mathematical equation and she calculated it. It clicked in her head, made sense. Wherever they had gone though, Em understood it was beyond her abilities to get there.

"You are correct, Em. There are many pockets between worlds and realities. I believe that human quantum mechanics addresses this concept as space-time, although it's more than that, and less than that."

Before Em could fully grasp that Aine had read her mind, another person came into the room.

"Aine, how lovely to see you."

Em turned and saw a woman so brilliantly beautiful that it hurt to look at her. The woman pursed her lips and turned her lights down a bit and Em was able to get a better view.

"You are a Charvez! Delightful. I met your sister, she's a strong one. Over the generations, you each inherit certain of my own gifts. With her, it's as if she got the biggest helping. My magic, my raw power. With you though..." Freya walked around her and examined her carefully, "you got my intuitive powers, my powers of translation and understanding. You feel, don't you? People and things, books, magic."

Em nodded. It was unreal, standing there in some alternate universe, talking to a goddess. She had so many questions!

"You haven't begun to tap into them fully, lovely girl. You must. Now that Aine," she looked up at the queen and winked, "that naughty girl, has made you Fae, you will be able to do so more easily. Your empathic abilities will be tenfold." Freya took her hand. "The shadow is still there. Your sister defeated part of the last threat but the threat remains."

"The demon lord," Em said matter of factly and Freya nodded. "What is it? What can I do to stop it? We got the book away, what else could it be?"

"Angra was not the only one who serves. Keep in mind, Em, that people serve the same master for a whole host of reasons."

"Okay, so you're saying the demon lord has more people out there trying to break the Compact. Who? How can I stop it if I don't even know where to look?" Em began to feel a bit panicked. Her family was at stake.

"I cannot be more specific. I am sorry but as I told your sister, there are rules that even I have to obey. Just be vigilant. Protect yours and be aware. That is the key." Freya kissed her forehead and Em felt a rush of pleasure.

"We should go, Em. Con is expecting us back and he is nervous about your safety, even with me," Aine murmured into her ear.

"Wait! I have so many questions to ask!" Em's natural curiosity burned through her. The desire to know, to learn and understand, was like an addiction for her and this goddess had to have so much to teach.

Freya laughed and Em had to close her eyes for a moment against the beauty of it. "Em, there will be other times. You're immortal now, you have thousands of years to learn. I will be here from time to time. For now, go to the man you love, a Joining awaits."

Aine grasped her hand and suddenly they were standing in a meadow ringed by thick forest and at the center a deep, clear lake. A beautiful home dominated the space. The transition from wherever Freya had been to Tir na nOg was a bit jarring and Em slowed her breathing down until it passed.

"This is Finn and Magda's home, Con's brother and his wife. I suspect his mother is here too, the snob," Aine sniffed.

"I take it you two aren't the best of friends," Em said quietly and Aine laughed.

"So refreshing. Please, do come and see me often or I will track you down myself. I will be going. As you have so astutely realized, Titania and I are not friends. She's always felt that I wasn't good enough to be queen. Too bad for her, I've been queen for sixty thousand years and I'm not dead yet. She's not a big lover of humans but she'll see, as I do, that Con is deeply in love with you. You two are fated and now you are no longer human anyway, you're one of us. Blessings upon the both of you," Aine said with a brief touch of her lips to Em's cheek and shimmered away.

Hearing laughter coming from the direction of the house, Em walked toward it. She came around the back of the house and saw the full expanse of the lake down a grassy embankment. It smelled so clean and fresh. She felt the joy and the love and it reminded her of her own family get-togethers.

A small boy with reddish-brown hair toddled toward her. "Hi, lady!" he called out gaily.

"Hi, mister," she called back with a smile. Con was standing nearby and turned when he heard her voice. The smile he gave her made her knees weak.

It wasn't until then that she noticed the small crowd of people who had all turned to look at her. The meadow suddenly exploded in flowers.

A woman with blonde ringlets came toward her as Con did. "You must be Em! I'm Magda, sister-in-law to Con." The little woman pulled her into an embrace. "You're even more beautiful than I'd imagined. I always wanted black hair, yours is the color of a raven's wing."

"Nice to meet you, Magda," Em said with a smile. There was a glimmer of mischief in Magda's eye and Em responded to it with a grin.

Con leaned down to kiss her lips and swing her around. "Em, *a ghra*, this is Finn, my older brother."

The other man was nearly identical to Con. The small differences were that his hair was a bit more red and rather than the whiskey gold of Con's eyes, Finn's were a startling ice blue. He grinned and kissed her cheeks. "Welcome to our home, Em. Welcome to our family and to our world. You've made Con so happy we can't help but love you already."

Em gave him a smile and before she could respond the small crowd parted and she was face-to-face with a regal golden blonde-haired woman who had to be their mother.

"Mother, this is Em. Em, this is my mother, Titania," Con said, giving his mother a look over Em's shoulder that she couldn't see.

Em could feel the other woman quite clearly. She thought Em was beneath her son but she also saw that fate had meant for the two of them to be together. Em gave a mental snort. It sucked when fate threw you the opposite of what you wanted.

"I'm very pleased to meet you, Con has spoken of you with great love and respect," Em said, holding out her hand.

The other woman gave her the once-over and gave a smile that didn't quite reach her eyes in return. "I'm pleased Con is happy," she said with a nod and moved back away.

Con narrowed his eyes at his mother but Em touched his arm to stop him from speaking. Her family had just savaged him the night before. It didn't matter, they were together and everyone would simply have to get used to it. She saw that Jayce was there and gave him a wave and her head spun as Con introduced her to the rest of the group.

Finally, he turned to her, "Em, last chance before I snap you up forever. If you haven't changed your mind, shall we speak the Joining?"

"Joining?"

"It's like a marriage." He hesitated a moment, looking for the right words. "Well, a bit more complicated than that. It's like a ritual, we speak the word and our souls weave together," he said, golden eyes twinkling.

"I'm game if you are," she said with a grin and he led her to the center of the group. Of course she couldn't wait to hear it, to learn a new spell and a new kind of magic.

"Finn will serve as *finné*, the witness," he said and his brother stepped forward and had them clasp hands and placed his over theirs.

"May the blessing of light be on you—light without and light within. May the blessed sunlight shine on you and warm your heart 'til it glows like a great peat fire."

Con smiled at his brother and then down at her. "*Tá mo chroí istigh ionat go deo.*"

And she understood. She didn't quite know why but the Gaelic was as understandable in her brain as English and French were. The spell was there, her part to speak came to her as if she'd known it all her life. She'd really have to marvel at that later. "My heart is within you forever as well, *fear cheile*," she repeated back.

"You do me a great honor to call me husband, *bean cheile*," he said in his silky voice.

She reached up to kiss his chin. "I like you calling me wife."

Finn grinned at them both. "Joined in light and in love for eternity and a day."

And it was as if he'd pulled her to him and into his heart and mind. She felt him like he was a part of her own heart. She looked up into his eyes and saw her face reflected there and understood that the spell had worked and that more than just a marriage of two lives, their very beings were joined to the other.

The gathered people cheered and Con swung her up into his arms with a whoop of joy and kissed her.

As the day wore on and the light changed, they danced through the flowers and Em got to know her new family and friends. She respected Con even more once she'd met the people in his life, and even his mother had warmed up to her as the afternoon passed.

Long after the stars began to wink in the sky Con grabbed her hand and shimmered them home.

"Thank you for such a lovely day," she said softly to him.

"Thank you, Em, for being my wife. You've won the hearts of all of my family and friends, you know," he said with a grin as he slid his hands down her thighs and then reversed, pulling the hem of her skirt upwards.

"Except for your mother."

"I'm sorry about that, but she's already beginning to come around."

She waved it off and her breath hitched as he reached the waist of her panties and tugged them down. "Let's not talk about her now," she moaned and he chuckled. "Show me if making love as a Fae is different than as a human," she challenged.

He fumbled with her blouse but it wouldn't cooperate and he took both hands and yanked it open, the buttons hitting the walls and the floor. Her eyes widened and then slid halfway shut, the sheer violence of his passion shocked her system and moisture flooded her pussy.

Her hands yanked frantically at his pants and she just imagined them both naked and they were.

"Nice," he growled as he leaned down to bite the flesh where neck met shoulder. His hands smoothed down her back and the curves of her ass. When his fingers brushed the wet flesh of her labia they both moaned. "So wet. Oh, Em, gods, you are so beautiful."

"All for you, Con, only for you," she gasped and practically climbed up his legs and wrapped her legs around his waist. "Fuck me, oh god, please, Con. I need you inside of me right now," she begged, moving her hips to graze his erection with her pussy.

Keeping an arm banded about her waist, with her ankles locked at the small of his back, he carried her into the bathroom. There were mirrors everywhere and he gave her a look so lethally sexy that she nearly died from it. "I'm going to fuck you in here so I can watch you in the mirrors. I want to see as my cock as it disappears into your body over and over, I want to watch that pretty flush work its way up your body, to watch your nails dig into the flesh of my shoulders," he said in a low voice, backing her against a full-length mirror on the wall. He surged into her and she arched her back and cried out in pleasure.

The fullness he gave her felt so good, so familiar. She was home. He was her home. She looked up into his face and smiled. "I love you, Con. I'm so glad you stalked me for six months."

He threw back his head and laughed, thrusting hard enough so that they both grunted. "I love you too, *mo fiach*, so much that it should scare a former confirmed bachelor like me."

She quirked a smile and then gasped as he licked across her collarbone. She leaned in and grabbed the tip of his ear between her teeth, flicking her tongue across it.

"Gods I love it when you do that," he murmured.

She watched him in the mirrors as he fucked her, his buttocks hollowing as he plunged inside, the muscles on his back rippling as he pulled back out again. She saw her breasts move from side to side with the motion. She watched his hand on her bottom, holding her up. It was a turn-on, watching him fuck her. She looked at herself and was surprised. Who was that woman, that sultry, wanton woman with her legs wrapped around this man's waist, begging him for more? She smiled and raked her nails down his back, delighting in the groan of pleasure he gave in response.

"Touch yourself for me, Em," he said, his eyes bright with passion.

She leaned back against the mirror and stroked her hands up her body, cupping her breasts. She felt him harden inside her as she did, eyes locked to her hands as her thumbs flicked over the nipples and then squeezed. She slid one hand down her stomach and stroked along his cock as he thrust into her and back up, finding the swollen bundle of her clit. She stroked it with a featherlight touch.

"That's it, baby, gods, you're so sexy," he gritted out, "I'm close, come with me, Em." He looked down in between them to watch her and she watched him watching her. She clamped down on his cock and felt his heartbeat throb inside her.

"Oh yeah. Like that. That. Feels. So. Good," he said, slamming his cock deep inside her.

As her climax hit, she began a long shuddering moan, the pleasure rippling over her like waves. She put her head on his shoulder and rode each crest. Her skin felt like a thousand fingertips were stroking it, the pleasure was wringing her out, pulling endorphins from her cells. It was nearly so much she couldn't stand it but she never wanted it to stop.

Con put his head on her shoulder and shuddered as his own climax hit and she felt his heart pounding against her flesh, his breath heavy.

Instead of putting her down as she'd expected he walked back into the bedroom and out onto the beach.

"Con! Hello, we're outside," she said, panicked.

He chuckled and walked into the water, her body still wrapped around his. "No one will see, no one lives out here. Even if they did they'd leave us alone. I want to be with you here in the Sea of Sighs with The Million Stars above our heads."

The water was warm and silky against her desire-heated flesh. It smelled clean and crisp and she took a deep breath. "It's really spectacularly beautiful here."

His face softened. He'd wanted so much for her to see the beauty of Tir na nOg, to want to be there, to find his world as bewitching as he did. "I'm glad you like it. Can you swim, Em?"

"Yes, of course…"

Before she could finish he tossed her into the waves and she came up sputtering and laughing. Her laughter died as she watched him, his body bathed in moonlight. The shadows on his skin, light glistening off the water on his flesh.

"You're so beautiful, Con," she whispered and reached for him. She shimmered them onto the sand and he created a fluffy blanket and sea of pillows on the seagrass. She shoved him onto his back and followed, sitting back on her heels as she watched him.

"Good job on the shimmer urghh…" he mumbled as she licked a line from his ankle to his groin. She gave a wicked chuckle and lapped around his sac, tasting the salt of the sea, the musk of his body.

She lapped up the long hard line of his cock and swirled her tongue over the head, catching the salty bead of pre-cum.

"Turn around," he whispered and she shook her head, not wanting to release his cock. "You're like a dog with a bone," he laughed as she refused to move, thinking he wanted her to stop sucking him. "Turn around so that I can taste you too."

She looked up the line of his body and raised a brow. He remembered her inexperience and helped her, guiding her body to where he needed it to be, pulling her open and sliding a thumb inside her. He felt a thrill of possession—she was his and no one else's, no other man had ever touched her this way, made her feel this way. He lapped at her, teasing every inch of her humid flesh, tasting her, devouring her, not allowing one drop of her honey to escape.

"Oh, oh…" she cried out, letting go of him as she came, legs trembling, grinding her pussy into his face.

Before she could take him into her mouth again he quickly moved her so that she was astride and slowly sinking down onto him.

Her head lolled back, her bottom lip caught between her teeth, gorgeous breasts thrust out just for him.

"Oh, Em, feeling you around me, clutching me like a greedy fist, I never want to leave you but at the same time, I want to slam into your pussy until I shoot my seed into you, branding you."

"No wonder you got so much action over the years, I'd take my panties off for a stranger with lines like that," she teased but he saw the tenderness shimmering in her eyes.

"That little scenario has possibilities. I'm the tall stranger, you're the shy virgin. You let me fuck you in your hotel room. Oh wait, we already played that one."

She blushed and then laughed with such joy that it floated on the air, the magic of Tir na nOg combined with her own newly given Fae magic and her inherent gifts made it a tangible thing. It fell down upon them like a warm rain and she raised her hands into the air to catch it as she rode him with relentless determination until he could bear her embrace no longer and came with a roar of her name that challenged the sea.

As the sun came up, Con carried her back inside and they fell asleep in their great big bed, limbs entwined.

* * * * *

Bron watched them from behind a dune. His loathing for Conchobar MacNessa and his human bride was obvious in the sneer he wore on his face. He'd been appalled to hear that the bitch queen had given the human the gift of the Fae. How dare that lowbreed human be allowed to ascend to their level!

He watched as they coupled under the waning moon and was shocked as the warm rain of her joy touched his face.

He felt the mark on his side burn and biting back a curse, sifted to another dimension to answer his summons.

"You took your time, Fae," the voice said. The voice was so harsh it was like chewing glass. It made Bron's skin crawl and his stomach cramp.

"Look, I got your call but I was checking some things out, I didn't want to waste my time until I had some answers. Our contact was right, the book is in Tir na nOg, in the queen's library."

"Why don't you have it?" the demon lord demanded.

"I can't just walk in there and take it, it's not a lending library and she's got magical wards laid on it anyway. No one can shimmer in or out and it's guarded by the Queen's Favored. I'll have to figure a way to get in there."

"You aren't going to disappoint me are you, Bron? You do know what happened to the last person who did that, don't you?"

Bron's pulse sped up at that. "Yes, the Charvez witch killed him and saved their precious Compact."

The demon turned in Bron's direction and he felt the full force of the dread and putrid stench that it emanated. He steeled himself not to flinch—he'd waited eight thousand years to revenge himself on Con MacNessa and those filthy humans, he wouldn't blow it now that he had a real chance.

"That book will enable me to break the Compact once and for all. It will divest the Charvez bitches of their power. I'll eat their souls and feed on the marrow of the bones of every human in New Orleans. And then I'll break down every other such Compact and their dimension will be a feast of fear and disease."

Bron shuddered at the thought. "I said I'd get it, it will just take time. I'll come to you when I have something else to report," he said and sifted out of there, eager to be away from the presence of the thing.

Chapter Twelve

Em awoke with a surprised gasp of pleasure, her back bowing off the bed. Con's face was between her thighs, his long hair gliding over her hips and legs. He shifted her thighs up and over his shoulders and she gave a squeal of delight when he sucked her clit into his mouth, gently grazing it with his teeth. She could hear how wet she was, the sounds of her own tortured breathing and of his tongue lapping and slurping at her.

"Oh god," she moaned long and hard as she came. Unceremoniously, she was tossed over and her ass hauled up so that he could slip into her from behind.

"Ahhh, gods, your pussy in my face and now gripping my cock, I've become addicted to mornings with you, *mo fiach*," he rumbled.

"Good," she squeaked out as he pistoned into her, her muscles still twitching from climax, the blanket of sleep still hanging over her consciousness. Her muscles were relaxed and he was warm and hard. Their room smelled like sex and the salt of the sea, it had imprinted on her brain and she'd forever associate that scent with her love for him.

After he'd come they lay together listening to the ocean. "I love you, Em."

"I love you, too, *fear cheile*."

"Your Gaelic is good."

"It's just there now. Freya said that the power I'd gotten from her was intuition and that language was part of it. She said that the change would heighten my powers. It's pretty cool to understand a language I'd never heard more than a few words of before I met you."

They went into the ridiculously large bathroom and he turned on the showerheads and drew her inside the gargantuan stall with him. Again, she couldn't help but look around at the place in awe. Hedonist that he was, he wasn't kidding when he said he liked a big bathroom for sex.

The ceiling was open with large skylights, real ivy scaled the walls and a gorgeous natural stone, much like malachite made up the counters and the interior of the shower. There were benches carved into the walls and multiple showerheads at different levels. She saw that the bathtub was the size of a Jacuzzi tub and she made a mental note to try that out soon.

He scrubbed her front and back, his large hands slippery as they slid over her breasts and tugged on her nipples. His caresses lingered on her behind and he placed her facing the wall of the shower, hands up above her head against the tile. He ran his slippery fingers over her nipples again and down into her pussy, spreading her legs with a gentle nudge of his foot. He stroked down the curve of her ass and spread her open, stroking a slippery finger over the puckered bud of her anus and she gasped and trembled.

"Em, I'd like to fuck you here," he said in her ear as his fingers continued to stroke over her. "May I?"

The taboo thrilled her even as it scared her. She trusted him without question so she tilted her hips, offering herself to him in answer.

She heard the lube splat into his hand and it dribbled down the crevice between her cheeks and pooled around her rear passage. He worked a finger inside her and she moaned low. "I've never done this before, Con."

She could hear his breathing get more ragged.

Her trust in him slammed into his chest. He hadn't thought it possible to love her more and yet he did at that moment as she gave herself to him once more.

"Of course you haven't, you're mine, *mo fiach*. I'm the first, the only and the last man who will ever be here. I only hope to be worthy of that honor. I'll be gentle, you'll like it but if you don't, I'll stop." He brought the tip of his cock to her entrance and she let out a slow breath as she tried to relax. "That's it, just relax, baby." He pushed in a bit and she felt the burning of his breach and the incredible sense of fullness as he eased in a bit and back out, in a bit more and back out. He put two fingers into her pussy and fucked her at the same pace.

"Oh, yes, that's nice," she moaned at the double penetration. Her nipples pressed against the cool stone walls, slippery with soap. He was in her, around her and over her. She felt totally possessed by him and it took her breath away.

The invasion of his cock in her ass wasn't painful but it wasn't quite pleasurable either. It felt full. He slowly worked himself in and out, crooning softly to her to relax. Once her muscles stretched to accommodate him the pain lessened and she could feel the intensity of nerves not used to being fired. It was overwhelming, but in a good way. He slid in all the way to the root and they both stilled, letting her body stretch around him that final bit. She could feel him pulsing, his fingers stroked her inner walls and she realized he was touching himself through the thin barrier between her pussy and anus. The thought of it turned her on so intensely that she started to come and reached down to move the heel of his hand against her clit. He moaned at that and began to fuck her with both his hand and his cock as she exploded around him.

"Oh, man. That's so good," he grunted, as she clamped down on him, her pussy spasming around his fingers, honey raining down onto his hand. Her cries of pleasure, the way her body clutched at him, it was too much and he began to come, his strokes choppy now instead of fluid. He put his forehead against her shoulder, breathing hard, his heart pounding against her back as he emptied into her.

He pulled out slowly and rinsed them both off gently, with such care that it made her chest hurt.

He looked up at her as he dried her off with soft circular strokes. "What did you think? Did I hurt you?" he asked.

"You didn't hurt me," she said as she kissed along his jawline. "It was intense but I liked it. Not something I'd do every day but something I'd definitely want to do again."

He grinned. "Good, now shall we take a tour?"

* * * * *

He took her through tropical forests and to rivers and lakes. They visited the western sea where his mother lived — although they avoided her home — as well as the northern shores, which were craggy and cold and dangerous-looking.

They ate a late lunch back at their home on the southern Sea of Sighs and she delighted in the differences in such a small island and said so.

His face got sad. "There are so few of us left. Once Tir na nOg teemed with the Sidhe but now we are but half of our old numbers."

"Why?"

"War, mainly. We don't get sick. We live in a society where there are more males than females, which leads to less population growth. We have such long lifespans that many times we do not mate until it appears to be too late. Fae females can and do have children after five thousand or so, my mother did at thirty thousand, but there seems to be a diminished fertility after about ten thousand."

"Con, where's your father? You've never spoken of him."

He sighed. "He died three thousand years ago. Murdered."

She looked at him with alarm. "Oh no! I'm so sorry, Con. How? Who?"

"Dark Fae," he saw the confusion on her face and explained, "sort of like your dark mages or practitioners of the dark path. They are those who hate humans and the fact that the Fae have protected them for millennia."

He stood up and began to pace. "My father was part of the Queen's Favored as well. As such, it was his job to keep the Fae in line with regard to their behavior toward and treatment of humans. A cop of sorts.

"Eight thousand years ago he executed one of us who'd been using one of our magical items to bespell humans and cause them harm. He'd been warned repeatedly to stop but he refused. After an entire village of humans was bespelled and several were killed, my father had to obey the queen's orders and track Aillen down and execute him.

"You've no idea how rare this is, Em. We don't kill each other, not the way humans do. Our wars have been with other beings. For a Fae to kill another Fae…it's a very difficult thing to bear. My father hated it but he did it. Not only because his queen ordered it but because it is one of our worst crimes to harm humans through magic.

"Three thousand years ago, the sons of Aillen and other members of the group of Dark Fae hunted my father and murdered him in revenge. Finn and I were with him that day. We'd been swimming and were laying on the sand to dry in the sun. I wanted a shave ice but not one that I conjured, I wanted to go to a place not too far away to get it from a stand. Because we can simply make things by will, handmade items are highly sought after here. My father didn't want to come so Finn and I went to get some for the three of us. They got him while we were gone.

"My selfish insistence over those bedamned ices got my father killed. I couldn't have just conjured something up with magic, no, I had to go and get something for the novelty," he said softly, the pain in his voice clear.

She stood up and went to him, blocking his pacing. "Oh, love, the bad guys killed your father, you wanting a shaved ice didn't cause that."

"If I'd been there, I could have protected him."

"You said your father was one of the Queen's Favored? That's like a squad of super warriors, right?"

He nodded.

"So, your dad, he got old and retired?"

"No. No, not at all. My father, even at sixty thousand, was hale and hearty and strong. He was still one of her strongest. Even at ten thousand I'm not half the warrior that my father was then...oh, you're trying to teach me a lesson..." he trailed off.

"Handsome and bright," she said as she stroked her hands up his arms. "They could have killed him on a day when he was alone. You guys can shimmer in and out at will, right? So it was just a stupid fate thing that led you to being there that day. You're no more to blame than Finn is."

"I miss him," he said brokenly and sat down, pulling her into his lap and holding her tight against him. "He taught me everything. Still, even after all of this time I have to catch myself when something momentous happens. I want to rush to him, to seek his advice or to share good news with him. Gods, he would have loved you."

"I wish I could have met him, Con. Where are these Dark Fae now? Did they get caught?"

"One of them did, one of Aillen's sons, and he was executed. I executed him. The rest haven't been caught. They have been making a comeback recently, claiming to want to heal the rift between us. But those that were part of the murder of my father are still wanted. When I finally catch them I'll kill the one who murdered my father and the others will be stripped of their magic and immortality by the queen and banished from Tir na nOg forever." He shuddered.

"Aine has that sort of power?"

He looked down at her with a puzzled smile. "You should work on calling her the queen or Your Majesty. Our culture is more formal in that way."

"She told me to call her Aine."

He lifted an elegant brow. "Really? Interesting."

"You call her Aine sometimes too, Con."

"Yes, well, sometimes. I've served her for nearly ten thousand years." And they'd been lovers for a brief time as well but he didn't feel the need to share that with his wife.

"Getting back to your original question, yes. She's the oldest of those who still live among the Fae anyway, and incredibly powerful. The spell of immortality is hers to administer. It can be used in reverse."

"I thought it was just some juice drink, some tonic."

"Her spell was made tangible. The drink was the spell. It's a rare thing that she did yesterday, Em. Over our entire history less than a hundred humans have been brought over."

"Wow, cool."

He quirked up a smile at that.

* * * * *

A few days later Em was summoned to the queen's chambers.

Once she arrived, she was shown into the queen's private chambers. Con, refusing to let her go unescorted, followed in her wake.

"Em, come in!" Aine exclaimed with a delighted clap of her hands. "Con, what on earth are you doing? I only invited your wife. You are not necessary."

He sputtered, trying to find something to say, not wanting to leave Em alone. She was so dear to him, so important that he couldn't bear the idea of losing her the way he lost his father. "Majesty, her powers are new, there are those here who do not wish her well."

Aine narrowed her eyes at him. "Are you saying that I would allow harm to come to your wife in my own court, Conchobar?"

He bowed but would not leave. "Of course not, Majesty, but she is my bride and I want to protect her."

Em heard the plea in his words and marveled at how a man so strong could love her so much that he would humble himself and be willing to invoke the wrath of the queen for her.

"Oh for the love of Brigid! Con, I've been around the world a few times, eh? There's not anyone here that is a match for me. I would never allow harm to come to Em. I can see that you are practically ready to throw yourself down and beg so you may stay in court but Em and I are going to have luncheon and take a tour around the gardens. It has been two thousand years since I've actually wanted the company of another woman just to chat with and you'll not ruin that with your presence. I'll have you summoned when we are done."

He looked at Em with a smile and she blew him a kiss and followed the queen out, taking a seat at a lovely table near a fountain. The surrounding garden was lush and bright with sensual scents.

"How are you liking Tir na nOg, Em?"

"It's really beautiful here. Con took me all over the island a few days back, showed me forests and mountain streams and all of the seas. I've never seen anything so lovely. The shimmering thing is pretty cool, too. I want to try to sift but Con wants me to work on shimmering for a while longer. I tried to explain to him that I understand the mechanics of it but he won't listen. Said it took him a year and that there was no way I could do it after a week."

"I'm sure you can do it, I can feel it. But Con, well, he's afraid to lose you. If you make the wrong calculation while sifting between worlds it could be disastrous. He lost someone special, it haunts him."

"He told me about his father."

"Nessa was an incredible man. I loved him deeply, I miss him to this day," Aine said, the mask of pain on her face clear.

"Loved him? Like a brother, loved him?"

Aine gave her a measuring look. "No, like a woman loves a man, loved him. Nessa was everything any woman could desire. He was mine before Titania came along. He was Con's age when we became lovers. Gods, he was incredible in bed. Made a woman remember why she was a woman. Exciting and tender. We were together for twenty thousand years.

"I was stupid and we broke things off. That's when he met Titania and the rest, as they say, is history. I was with Con a few times…he reminds me so much of his father but the spark wasn't there. It's never been there with anyone else."

"I knew it!" Em said with a smirk. "Today he gave me a lecture about calling you Your Majesty, and then I told him you'd said to call you Aine and mentioned that he sometimes called you Aine and then he got all nervous."

Aine laughed. "It really wasn't a big deal and it was two thousand years ago anyway. Just a few weeks, both of us grieving for his father. You have nothing to worry about. I'd hate for you to feel uncomfortable, I do so enjoy your company."

Em smiled at Aine. "Three months ago I would have felt panicked, I'm all right now. I know he loves me. I'm sorry about Nessa. From the way you and Con speak of him he sounds like an amazing man."

"He always stayed at my side, even after he'd married Titania. Threatened to leave once, after I'd tried to seduce him back into my bed. Told me he'd made a life with Titania. By then they'd had Finn, and he wouldn't have betrayed that. It made me love him even more, the fool." She smiled up at Em.

Em reached out and squeezed Aine's hand. Aine looked surprised and then touched. "I haven't been touched like that, out of genuine friendship, since I was very young. Thank you, Em." Aine stood up and gestured around the garden. "As a boon for your friendship, ask anything of me and it's yours."

"Aine, you don't need to reward me for my friendship, that's free of charge."

"You see, an old queen can learn a few new things. I do not wish to insult you by making such an implication. How about this, would you care to see the library? My private library?"

Em's eyes gleamed and Aine laughed with delight.

"Come then, let's go," she held out her hand and Em grabbed it. They walked through the gardens into another part of the house, castle, keep, whatever it was, and down a long hallway.

Em could feel the magics protecting the place. She watched as Aine's hands moved, undoing them as they passed. Em turned up her own magic, casting out to see what she could feel in the spelled hallway.

It was fairly quiet as they walked together. Em could feel the guards at the other end and some faint glimmerings of emotion floating on the air. But as they neared the doors at the end, Em felt something in the pit of her stomach. "Something is wrong," she murmured and Aine stopped.

"What do you mean?" Aine demanded.

"There's someone here who isn't right. I can't explain it. You all feel a certain way, this is not the same."

Aine relaxed. She was confident in her own spells and her people. "I'm sure it's that there are books here that contain some of the oldest dark magic in the worlds, as well as our own magical historical texts. That's probably it."

Em nodded, relieved but feeling dubious. She was still adjusting to her new level of power since she'd taken the spell the week before and she knew Aine was incredibly powerful. Talking herself into being mistaken and confused by the magical texts, they walked through the double doors and Em lost her thoughts as she took in the sight. She gasped, the room was simply magnificent. She could feel the magic humming in the air and as Aine had said, she felt the currents of the positive and negative magic swirling about her.

Em wandered the rooms, fingertips caressing the spines of the books. She heard the voices of thousands of beings older than recorded human time. She was in heaven.

"Aine, these are breathtaking. If I lived here, I'd end up sleeping in here at night," she said with a laugh and Aine smiled.

"Here then, look at the book you found for us after it had been lost for so many years." Aine handed her *The Shifting Veil*. Em read through it, amazed that she was able to understand it all.

They spent a few hours there, Aine delighting in Em's appreciation for the magical history of the Fae.

"I am so glad that you are pleased. I will leave notice with the guards that you are to be granted admittance at any time you wish. You can't sift or shimmer into these rooms, or even the hallway. It's warded against that. Feel free to come any time you want."

"Oh thank you, Aine! What a lovely gift."

"And you waste it on this human filth."

Em turned around just in time to see Aine slump to the ground. She looked up and saw a tall, blond man with rugged features holding a heavy wall sconce. "She may have a lot of power, but she can't fight a blow to the back of the head. And you, well, you can't fight that either. Immortality won't save you from a crushed skull. Oh how Conchobar will grieve for you, knowing that he left you to be murdered just like his father was, on his watch."

"You're Dark Fae!"

"Astute for a human," he said indolently.

She turned her mind inward and saw the wards which blocked shimmering and sifting. She reached out and began to unravel one. It wouldn't allow her to go very far but if she could just escape this room she'd have a chance to save her life and the life of the queen. She untied it like she did the knotted Christmas tree lights in her parents' garage each year.

"I'm not a human, you know. I'm immortal too." She wanted to keep him talking until she could open a space in the wards.

"Your ears show your birth. You may have been granted immortality by the queen but you still come from human stock. It's really too bad you were so baseborn. If you were Fae and common, I'd make you mine in a second. Con will most certainly miss you in his bed. But that will only push him into madness quicker, which is just fine."

She almost had it. "What is your glitch anyway? Why are you angry at Con?"

"His father killed my father for daring to act like the god he was. Because he didn't bow and scrape to the humans he was executed. And then his son, your precious Conchobar, killed my brother. That family has ruined mine and they'll pay. He'll lose his loved ones as I lost mine."

She shimmered and caught the beginning of his roar of frustration.

She ended up in the audience chambers and began to scream for help. Jayce was the first person she saw that she knew. He ran to her and grabbed her arms.

"What is it? Em, are you all right?"

"The queen, she's been knocked out in her library. Hurry, there's a Dark Fae there, Aillen's son!" she explained hastily.

Con shimmered into the room, feeling her distress now that they were joined. He shoved Jayce out of the way and pulled her into his arms. "Em, gods, are you all right? What's happened?"

"We've got to get into the library." Jayce grabbed them both and shimmered to the end of the hallway where the wards started and then ran before she could even tell him that she'd untangled the wards.

Em reached out but the dark feeling in the pit of her stomach was gone. "He's gone!" she called out, running behind Jayce and Con.

"Go back, Em! Damn it, you could get hurt," Con growled as they reached the doors.

"I'm not going anywhere, she's my friend."

They burst into the rooms and others came in behind them. A healer of some kind attended the queen.

"You can shimmer her out, there's a hole in the wards," Em said and the healer looked surprised but they shimmered out.

"What happened here, Em?" Jayce asked.

"She was showing the library to me. I love books and she wanted to share this." Em looked around the room and noticed the space where Aine had shown her the book Con had brought back. "Shit! The book! Con, he took it!"

"What book? Who?"

"I think it was Aillen's son. He said your father had taken his and that you had taken his brother and he was going to rob you of those you loved. He was going to k-k-kill me," she said, the realization of what could have happened suddenly hitting her.

He pulled her tight against him.

"He took *The Shifting Veil.*"

Con pushed her back so that he could look in her face. "Are you sure?"

"Aine, the queen, she showed me the book before he came in. It's not there now."

"How did he get in here and how did you get out?" a dark-haired man demanded of her.

"I don't know how he got in here. As to how I got out, I saw the wards and I unraveled one of them, a short one, and shimmered into the audience chamber."

"We're supposed to believe that a human broke one of the queen's wards? And at the same time as someone else figured out a way around them? This after they'd been unbreached for thousands of years? Do you think us fools?"

"Are you accusing my wife of conspiring with Dark Fae to kill the queen and steal the book?" Con demanded.

Jayce stepped forward and stood at Em's other side.

"She's the one who tracked the book down so that we could get it back, Poul! Why would she do that only to conspire to steal it?" Jayce demanded.

Em closed her eyes and focused. There were so many people in the room, so much background noise from their thoughts and feelings as well as the virtual ocean of magic ebbing and flowing from the books. Why was this man so angry with her?

Her eyes flew open. "You're one of them," she said softly.

Con jerked his head and faced her. "What?"

"He's one of them, the Dark Fae."

"Poul? He may be an arrogant ass but he's not a traitor. You've got to be mistaken, Em," Con said.

"What makes you say that, Em?" Jayce asked.

"Why are we even wasting time with this? She's a traitor and she's trying to throw blame my way," Poul sputtered.

"They feel different than you do. Even the Fae that hate and resent me, all at the base, feel the same. The Dark Fae, they give off this...well, they make me sick in the pit of my stomach. They just don't feel right," she told Jayce.

"We've got to kill her," Poul said.

"What? Oh no, you don't!" Con said.

The room was dividing and Em could see that there was going to be a tricky couple of minutes to come. It could go either way at the moment.

"She killed the queen!" another Fae called out.

"She did not!" Jayce said.

Em gave a shrill cabbie whistle and the room quieted. "Jesus! People, the BOOK is gone! Who has it and where is it? Shouldn't we be out trying to find it? Put me in jail or whatever if you have to but find that book! My family could be harmed with that book, the innocents we protect are in danger."

"Kill her. Who cares about that book?" Poul said.

Con's eyes gleamed. "If you so much as think about killing my wife again I'll kill you with my bare hands. She found the book, she is the one who made sure I got it to bring back here. If she'd wanted to use the book for ill, she could have. She cooperated with me every moment. She has a pure heart.

"As for who cares about the book, your queen does. She's the one who sent me to watch over Em in the first place. She wanted that book back here in safekeeping, out of hands that could use it for ill."

"Only on humans. Why do we care what happens to them? And anyway, the queen sent you to watch this creature because she didn't trust her, so why should we?"

"Because I do."

They all turned and saw Aine standing there and the whole room bowed. Em went to her and hugged Aine tightly.

"Are you all right? I was so worried about you."

Aine smiled. "Just a bump on the head. Bron has a lot to learn about rendering a killing blow."

With a last smile at Em she turned her gaze out into the crowd. "You dare speak of killing one of my subjects without an order from me?"

"Majesty, we believe her responsible for the attack on you," Poul said.

"Why on earth would you think such a ridiculous thing?"

"She found a way around your wards at the same time that this Dark Fae found his way around them. It can't be coincidence."

"It isn't a coincidence."

Everyone gasped, including Con, who put his hand out and pushed Em behind his body.

Aine saw and laughed. "My sweet Con, I have no desire to harm my dear friend. What I meant was that I did not redo the wards as I walked down the hall toward the library when she and I first came in. Anyone with a half-decent ability to lay a detection spell would have known when the wards went down. As for Em finding her way around my wards, I know. She's got a knack for it. She sees the magic and understands it somehow. It's her gift. A gift that saved my life. And to address your incorrect comment, Poul, the Fae have compacts and covenants we are beholden to as well and the book, if used by the wrong people, is a danger to us as well as humans."

"Majesty, I believe you're making a mistake. To not kill this human will be your undoing," Poul said vehemently.

"No, Poul, your insistence on it is yours. How long have you been with them, Poul?" Aine asked, her words laced with a compulsion spell so strong that Em felt the crack of its power yank at her.

Poul went to his knees, struggling not to speak, his eyes screwed shut, mouth gaping open and snapping shut. "Die, human lovers!" he cried out and suddenly was holding a silver knife that he stabbed himself in the neck with before anyone would move.

He slumped over and fell to the ground, dead.

A panicked murmur filled the room.

"One of the Queen's Favored was Dark Fae. If Bron has the book, I have a feeling that he was informed of it by Poul. What is his plan?" Jayce asked no one in particular.

Em touched his arm. "Thank you, Jayce. When no one else believed me about Poul, you asked me to explain why I felt the way I did."

"There is no way Con would have married a woman who wasn't honorable and from what I've seen, you have a great talent for understanding people." He shrugged with a gentle smile.

"Freya! Something Freya said to me the other day. She said that the demon lord had other servants and that people serve for different reasons. Oh god, Bron is going to give that book to the demon lord. I've got to get home right now!"

Aine grabbed her arm before Con could do it. "Em, you can't be sure of that."

"Yes, I can. I know it."

"You can't put yourself in danger, Em," Con demanded.

"I will not stay here while my family is in danger. I can sift back myself if you won't help me but I won't sit and do nothing."

"Jayce, you go with them," Aine said to him and turned back to Em. "We can only have so many Fae in your realm at one time. I have my own compacts to adhere to. Take Jayce, he has great powers and is nearly as strong as Con." She pressed a kiss to Em's forehead. "Be well and come back soon, friend."

Con gave the queen a glare but saw that Em would go one way or the other. Sighing, he held out his hands and Em took one while Jayce took the other.

* * * * *

They sifted onto the sidewalk in front of Lee's house, ran through the gate and burst into the foyer of Lee's house. Em immediately yelled for her sister.

"What?" Lee's face poked out of the hallway upstairs. Her face lit with surprised delight at seeing her sister. "Oh! Em!" Lee ran downstairs and pulled her sister into an embrace.

"Honey, you look worried, what is it?" She looked at Con with narrowed eyes. "Did you hurt my sister again?"

He put his hands up in defense but before he could say anything Em interrupted. "No! He's not the problem. The book, the book I gave back to the Fae—it's been stolen. I think that the Fae who stole it took it to the demon lord."

Lee's face grew tense. "How do you know?"

"I just do. He stole it. Freya said that another served the demon lord. It makes sense that it would be Bron serving him, it, whatever pronoun is appropriate for a demon."

"We shouldn't jump to conclusions," Lee said. "We don't know that he stole it for the demon lord."

"Oh for god's sake! I just TOLD you that he did. I know he did. You're not the only one with gifts, Amelia Charvez! My gift says that Bron stole it for the demon lord. Bron hates Con and he hates humans, he stole a book that will enable the demon lord to unravel the Compact. That will divest you of your power and leave the innocents unprotected. Even if I didn't have the gift of intuition, common sense could put two and two together."

"You're right. I'm sorry. I just don't want it to be true. We've been waiting for the other shoe to drop all of this time. So tell me why you think it's true."

Em swallowed her anger, mollified by Lee's statement. Jayce and Con had taken a step back during the brief, angry exchange and now relaxed and gave a brief nod of hello to Alex and Aidan, who'd come to stand in the hallway behind Lee. "Okay, I get that. But as you are so fond of saying, I am a scholar and I've spent years doing research on dark magic and nearly a year's worth on this very book alone. This book has the power to create chaotic magic. It can unravel the foundations of magical agreements. I know the danger this book poses, I know the danger this Fae poses and I know that Bron MacAillen is in league with the demon lord and is out to use that book to hurt this family."

"She's right. The queen wanted the book back for that very reason. Your family isn't the only group in danger from the magic in the book, all compacts and agreements based on magic are, including ones that the Fae have entered into," Con said, putting a hand on Em's shoulder, feeling her tension ease at his touch. He hadn't jumped on her claim that Poul had been Dark Fae earlier when Jayce had. It wasn't that he hadn't believed in her power, but that he was shocked by the very idea that any of the Queen's Favored could be a traitor. When she'd thanked Jayce for believing her right away, Con had felt ashamed. He wanted her to know he supported her completely.

Lee sighed. "I do believe you. I just don't want it to be true. Losing *Tante* Elise was just so awful, along with nearly losing Alex and Aidan. I don't want to live that again."

Em nodded and the sisters hugged and the four men let out a long sigh of relief.

"Well, what do we do?" Lee asked.

"We wait. If what I recall is correct, the demon lord or his servant will have to face you to break the Compact. He'll need your blood. If we can hold him off then grab the book, we may be able to vanquish him this time." Em looked to her sister. "You think you're up to vanquishing a demon lord?"

"Hell no! Who the heck is ever up to something like that?" Lee said, pushing her hair out of her face. "We need to get *Maman* over here, two witch dreamers are better than one. She and I can dreamwalk to see if we can't locate this Bron and figure out what he's up to."

Lee went to the phone while Em introduced Alex and Aidan to Jayce. A month and a half had passed while they were away this time and even though it had only been a week for Em, she'd missed New Orleans and her family quite a bit. Despite their overbearing nature, they were still her family.

"*Maman* will be here in a few minutes. Let's get something to eat while we wait," Lee said.

Aidan winked at Lee, gave a mischievous grin and looked at Em. "It's been a very long time since I've tasted Fae blood, would you share yours with me?"

"NO!" Con bellowed and Em jumped. Lee smiled at Con's possessiveness.

"Aidan, I really don't want you to make my sister come. I know it's just food to you but still, there are lines a girl doesn't want to cross with her sister," Lee said dryly, going along with the tease.

"He makes you come just by feeding?" Em asked, fascinated.

Lee gave a smile and took Em's arm as she led her from the room. "Yes! And let me tell you…"

The conversation trailed off as Con scowled at Aidan.

"Oh, please, Con. I don't desire Em that way. She's a beautiful woman but she's my sister! I love Lee and no other woman makes me feel lust. I just wanted her blood, the climax is just a pleasant side effect." Aidan said with a smirk. He would have liked a sip of Em's blood but truthfully, he'd fed from Alex and Lee earlier and was quite sated, he'd just felt like twitting Con to see his reaction. He was pleased to see the Fae so possessive of his bride.

Several minutes later their mother arrived with the other Charvez women in tow, guarded by a coterie of men.

Em stood forward. "*Maman*, you and Lee should dreamwalk. I will ride with you." She turned to her brother-in-law. "Alex, I think you should as well. The rest of you should just keep an eye out, be on guard. Simone," Em said, turning to her cousin who was also an empath, "you will feel the difference if this Fae approaches. Jayce and Con feel a certain way, yes?" Simone nodded. "These Dark Fae, they give you that feeling in the pit of your gut that the dark ones bring."

Simone nodded again, understanding exactly what Em meant.

They turned back to Lee and her mother, who'd drawn a protective circle. Em and Alex stepped into it and the circle was closed. The room gave off a bit of electric shock as the magic was focused.

Alex and Em each put a hand on the shoulders of the witch dreamers and Con felt the magic roll through the room as they cast their consciousness outward.

Em watched as her sister and mother traveled in dreams, hovering just above the collective unconsciousness of those in the surrounding area. She kept her senses peeled for anyone who gave off the signature that the Dark Fae seemed to emanate.

They saw nothing, but Em felt a faint darkness, the stench of something truly evil just beyond their vision. The coldness of it seemed to slide down her spine, making her slightly nauseated. After a time they came back to themselves. Em looked at her mother and sister and stopped them as they began to break the circle.

"No. Wait." Em looked about and then to Simone. "Did you feel anything out of the ordinary?" she asked her cousin.

"There is something not quite right but I can't put my finger on it. It isn't close enough for me to really get a lock on." Simone shrugged.

"It's here, but they are just out of our range. I can feel it but it's as if they are behind a wall."

"Why can't we break the circle?" Lee asked.

"You're the key, Lee. As the current witch dreamer, as the strongest of us, you are the focus of the Compact and the one that the spell must be cast upon to break it."

"How do you know this, *mo fiach*? The book is not in your language," Con said.

Em shrugged. "I read it today before he took it and I did the research. It just...I can't explain it but it just made sense to me. Like with sifting, as it's happening I just understand it. I want to be sure that this demon lord isn't nearby before we break the protective circle."

She looked around again. "*Maman*, let me out but reseal the circle when you do."

"No! Damn it, Em! Do you think it's here and if so, why the hell do you want to put yourself in danger?" Con demanded.

"I'm not in danger, well, I mean, we all are, the entire city is if the Compact gets broken, but it's Lee and *Maman* who are at greatest risk. I just can't feel as much inside of the circle, it keeps magic out. I need to hear better and it has to be done outside this protective circle."

Con gave an exasperated sigh and Aidan patted his arm. "They're all like that, Con. You may as well get used to it now. There's enough magic in this room to protect her. Let her do her job."

Em smiled and stepped out of the circle and felt it close behind her. "The wards, they're so strong, I'm going to go to the door."

Con and Jayce followed her along with *Grandmere* and Simone. Em opened the door and took a deep breath and closed her eyes, letting her shields come down. The sheer volume of sensation made her take a step back, Con put his arms around her and she leaned back into him, reassured. She felt the wall, knew somehow that it was holding the presence of Bron and his master out.

She looked at it, examining it, figuring it out. She walked back inside and closed the door.

"He's here, as is the demon. They're using a spell of concealment. I can see it but I don't have the magic to break it."

"Em what if we join and you can guide me to it, I can take your knowledge and we can break the spell that way?"

"That just might work, Lee. We'll have to be ready for whatever gets thrown our way."

"You don't think we should just wait for them to make the first move?" Lee asked.

"The longer they have the book the more dangerous it is for us. We need to get that book back and to vanquish the demon once and for all." Em looked toward the door. "They're getting closer. I can feel them now, even through the wards. Shall we try this or not?"

Lee held out her hand and Em got back into the circle. Lee looked to Alex. "Honey, make a protective circle for everyone in the room. I want all of you to get inside of the circle and don't break it, no matter what."

"I'm coming in there with you, Em," Con said determinedly and he came in as Alex walked out.

"Lee, let's open up a hole in the wards to let them in and then *Maman*, you close them, locking them inside. If we aren't successful, at least the wards will hold them for a while," Em said.

Lee nodded and as soon as the other circle had been closed, she turned to her sister and pulled out a cutting blade and sliced her palm, her mother's and then Em's. She wrote symbols on their arms and spoke ritual words and felt the link form. Of witch dreamer to Em's particular kind of intuitive magic. She was something more than just an empath and together, the three of them formed an incredibly powerful unit. Lee was amazed at how much her sister knew, how much she felt and her respect and admiration for her grew knowing Em swam through that level of data every moment of the day. She understood what Em had been talking about regarding the wall around the others and put that in reserve as she focused on the wards, opening a hole and then stepping back to wait.

She didn't have to wait very long. Through her link with Em she felt the approach, and the miasma of the demon lord's power made her stagger. Em held her hand out and she joined with her sister and her mother. The power flowed through them like a live circuit and Alex watched with cautious eyes, taking it all in, waiting and ready to aid in any way he could from the other circle.

"They're coming," Em whispered and Con stepped in front of them and pulled out a deadly looking sword.

"Remember, *a ghra*, Bron is responsible for killing my father. He is my *namhaid*, my enemy. Let me take care of him. Know that there is no way he's getting near you. He will not harm you while I have breath."

She quirked up a corner of her mouth in a smile. "Do what you gotta do, big guy."

He snorted a laugh and turned back around.

The air shimmered and suddenly Bron and the demon burst into the room. The demon had cloaked his appearance and was looking like a human, er, sort of like a used car salesman from those old television commercials back in the Seventies, Em thought, distracted and felt Lee's momentary amusement at the thought. She also felt her mother begin to knit the hole in the wards back together.

"Nice work on breaking the concealment spell, witch," Bron said and looked at Con. "Conchobar MacNessa, it's a shame to see you hiding behind a witch's circle. Are you afraid of me?"

Con barked a laugh that was so menacing that it made the hairs on Em's arms stand on end. She knew the level of his grief over his father's death but she hoped it wouldn't make him stupid. Bron MacAillen was one thing. The dude in the polyester suit standing behind him was another. The evil rolled off him in waves — it made Em nauseated.

"Demon, begone from my home and from this realm," Lee said calmly.

Em studied them, waiting.

"I have waited hundreds of years to be free of the geas the bitch goddess put on me, to be rid of you once and for all. Angra failed but then your sister there did my homework for me and found the very tool of her family's destruction." The demon pulled out the book. "Ah, the irony of it all. I plan to kill them all one by one so that I can feast from your guilt and grief as you watch, helpless," it said with a slimy leer and Em's skin crawled. Her mother squeezed her hand in reassurance.

"Oh jeez, are you going to talk us to death or what? What is it with you bad guys anyway? I've never heard so much B-movie dialog in my life!" Lee said and Em barked out a laugh.

"I feel like we're in that Michael Jackson video for 'Beat It'. Think we're gonna rumble?" Em said and she and her sister sang the words and imitated the choreography, laughing at the blank look on the face of the demon.

Aidan shot a look at Con who just shook his head while Alex rolled his eyes.

The demon growled. "Oh, sorry. It's just that, well, I mean, I'm sure you're scary and all, I can feel the ickiness flowing from you, but your disguise, well, you look like a late-night television commercial circa 1977. Isn't that robin's egg blue plastic suit kinda uncomfortable?" Em asked and Lee burst out laughing again.

The demon continued to look perplexed by them.

"Uh, I don't think he gets it, Em," Lee said and sighing looked back to the demon. "So, Leisure Suit Larry, do you and your little dog Toto have something to awe us with or did you just plan to make us pass out from your stank?"

"Good one," Em said.

Their mother sighed. "You two, behave and focus on your work, please." She turned back to the demon and Bron. "I never could get them to stop with the wisecracks."

It was Con's turn to laugh.

"Prepare to die, witches, I will enjoy sucking the marrow from your bones," the demon said and everyone laughed.

Em was glad to have lightened the moment. Beneath the jokes she could feel her mother and sister's fear. It was impossible not to be terrified when you knew what was at stake.

The demon roared and shook off the disguise. He was truly horrifying to behold and everyone got quiet for a moment.

"Wow, much better, Larry," Lee said. "But two words for you — dental care."

Even Bron had to hold back a laugh then.

"Here it comes," Em whispered. "I'm going to look inward and focus, I'll feed you what I find out. Be ready because the magic he unleashes will begin to work immediately."

Lee and her mother squeezed Em's hand and Con did some wicked cool move with the sword, slicing the air, causing Bron to wince. Jayce did the same in the other circle.

Before they could do anything else, the demon impaled Bron on a long talon and he slumped to the ground with a surprised look on his face.

Con started forward. "CON! NO!" Em shouted and he stopped.

The demon laughed and the sound was truly horrifying.

Bron looked up at it. "You promised," he croaked.

"I lied."

It opened the book and began to speak. Em saw the magic flow out of its mouth. It appeared to her inner eye like a geometry problem. She hated geometry but gave a second's worth of thanks to her father for insisting on that tutor. She began to weave her way through it, sensing its makeup, the cornerstones of its construction. Lee picked up on it and began to aim her own defensive magic there. Alex used his magic to attack the demon, trying to keep it at less than full strength.

Em felt her sister's magic begin to get weaker and her mother chimed in, doubling back on the spell Lee was working to combat the chaotic magic. The problem was that the very nature of the spell the demon was weaving was that it was anti-magic magic, like a double logic puzzle. Each move caused a countermove that brought the spell back, zipping around the defense.

Em burrowed deeper into the magic to try and figure out a way to fight back that would end up making Lee even stronger. She felt her sister and mother getting weaker, the demon's spell getting stronger. She had to force that to the back of her mind as she burrowed deeper, examining the magic until she saw the answer.

"Repeat everything it says, counter the spell with the spell!" she said to Lee urgently.

Lee looked wary and then took a deep breath and nodded, trusting her sister.

The spell got stronger and Lee faltered. "Don't stop! Damn it, Lee, trust me," Em urged.

Their mother sent her power through Em and into Lee and Lee gave a last burst, meeting the spell the demon was laying, copying his words, his intent. Suddenly the magic became bright, intense. They all felt the magic being sucked from them and then just as suddenly it came rushing back, filling Lee and her mother up to overflowing.

The demon faltered and the magic, not having a place to go, began to drain out of it and into the witches in the room.

"Now! Vanquish it now or it'll be too late!" Aidan yelled.

Con walked out of the circle and Em yelled for him but Lee and her mother held her tight, making her stay in the circle, Lee continuing the spell and Alex working his magic to weaken the demon. Jayce broke through the other circle and together he and Con approached the demon.

It looked up and saw them approach. Jayce raised his sword but the demon lashed out with its magic. Con used the demon's split in concentration and plunged the sword into the neck of the demon as Jayce hit the wall. The demon screamed in pain and panic and Lee continued the spell, her mother joining Alex in the vanquishing spell.

The demon, spewing some kind of ichor, grabbed Con, who gave a scream of his own but Jayce was there and suddenly the demon had no head. A sickening thud sounded as the decapitated body hit the ground.

Lee broke the circle but kept connected to Em and her mother. They sprinkled salt on the demon's body as Alex and Marie completed the vanquishing spell. The demon's body shimmered out of existence.

Em pulled free and ran to where Con was slumped on the ground. "I've got to get him back home, the healers there can help him," she said and without thinking, sifted them back to Tir na nOg, to Aine's chambers.

Chapter Thirteen

ଅଠ

Aine looked up as they sifted back. "Help! He's been injured by the demon!" Em screamed and Aine moved toward them quickly, calling out for a healer.

The healers shimmered in, moved him to a bed and looked him over. Jayce showed up with Em's mother. "She wouldn't let me leave without her. She said you would need her," Jayce told her.

Marie pulled her daughter to her while they watched the healers work on Con.

"He's suffered some extensive injuries. We can often heal quickly from injuries caused by humans or other Fae, but something of great evil and power—something as old as this demon was—well, we'll see what we can do," the healer said.

"Just make him better, damn it, or you'll have me to answer to!" Em yelled and her mother hugged her. Jayce stood on her other side.

Titania and Finn shimmered into the room and Jayce quietly explained the situation to them. Finn kissed Em's forehead and introduced himself and his mother to Marie. Marie and Titania had a brief stare down until Titania nodded her head and put a hand to Em's face.

"He will survive this, Em. He's a strong man and he loves you. He won't walk away from you without a fight," she said softly and Em nodded, tears in her eyes.

They watched for hours as the healers worked. Con remained unconscious. The demon had attacked his life force. His system had shut down to protect his life force from being stolen or destroyed by the demon.

Finally, as the day ended, the healers stood back and began to move away from him. "We've done all that we can, his injuries have been dealt with. It's all a matter of his spirit reviving," the healer told Aine and shimmered out.

Em went to Con's side and grabbed his hands. "You'd better wake up, Con MacNessa, you made me immortal and changed my life. I can't live without you so wake the hell up and do it now!" She crawled into the bed beside him and wrapped her body around his, talking to him the whole time.

The others watched, feeling helpless, but Em continued to talk to him, urging him to wake up, telling him her plans to remodel their houses, talking of plans for a child, for learning to use her new Fae powers and going back to New Orleans for Mardi Gras.

She talked until she was hoarse and exhausted and finally she passed out, her face buried in his neck.

A day passed, then two, then a week. Jayce took Marie back home with a promise to keep them all apprised of the situation. They moved Con back to their house on the sea. Jayce insisted on staying there, each of them able to support the other when they began to lose hope.

* * * * *

Two weeks had passed and Con was still unconscious. Em woke up on yet another morning to find him still out. She rolled out of bed and looked down on him, angry. "Damn it! Conchobar MacNessa, what the fuck? Wake up! How dare you do this to me? All my life I've felt like no one really understood me, appreciated me, saw me as someone special apart from my family. You come along and hold up a mirror and you helped me to see myself, believe in myself. You have no right to let go of life and leave me here alone!"

She got rid of her nightshirt and lay on top of him, her naked flesh to his naked flesh. "Do you feel this, Con? Do you feel my skin against yours? Do you remember what it's like between us? Even now when you're unconscious I'm wet for you."

She kissed his neck, up to his ears, nibbling the point, flicking her tongue across it. "I know you're in there somewhere. Come back to me, baby. Come back, *fear cheile*, husband. I need you," she whispered and kissed down his ear, down his neck and across his jaw. She breathed him in, felt the pulse at his neck and bit down over the tendon there and he jumped.

"Con? Come on, baby, I love you so much."

She continued south, licking over his pebbled nipples and down over each rib and across the hard, flat stomach. His cock was hard now and hot against her flesh. She took biting nips at his lower abdomen and then breathed across his cock head before she took it into her mouth. She tasted the salty pearl of pre-cum and ran her nails down his ribs and underneath his butt, gripping his muscled ass.

She groaned and got wetter, missing him, aching with desire and love and grief. She took his cock deeper, wet her fingers with her own juices and tickled his rear passage. She slowly pushed her fingers inside until she found his prostate and stroked over it. His cock hardened to steel and she slowly stroked into him as she moved her mouth over him, pouring her love and her hope into the act, willing him to come back to her.

Suddenly he came and she was filled with the salty taste of him, with the essence of life, and tears sprang to her eyes as she heard him roar.

She was on her back and he was over her, sliding inside her, looking down at her wearing a look of such intense love and adoration that she began to weep as he stroked into her hard and deep. She wrapped her legs about his waist and tightened herself around his cock.

"You're awake," she said, breathless.

"I've heard you these last weeks. It was the only thing that held me to this plane. I only wish you'd thought of sucking my cock before now. Apparently there aren't blowjobs on the next plane of existence and my cock brought me back," he said with a grin and then sobered. "I felt so far away, I didn't know how to get back. All I could do was hold on and not let go. Each day I moved back a tiny bit closer. Your voice and your love were my anchor, Em."

She laughed through her tears and cried out as he latched onto a nipple and grazed his teeth across it. Her climax exploded through her system, jettisoning her fear, her anger, her grief and replacing it with his love and his life.

A few minutes after they'd both come and were wrapped around each other in their bed, she kissed his chest over his heart. "I've got to tell Jayce so that he can tell your mother and Finn. He went to see Aine. He gives her daily reports on your health. We've all been so worried about you."

He ran his fingers through her silky hair and brought her lips down to his.

Chapter Fourteen

ℰℛ

Con tapped a foot to the zydeco band and drank his beer while he watched Em dance with her brother, a beatific smile on her face.

"It's good to have you back," Jayce said quietly.

"It's good to be back," Con replied. "I couldn't imagine death without her. Thanks for being there for her while I was out."

"You're the brother of my heart—that makes her my sister. Plus, if you'd kicked, I could have snapped her up," he joked and Con scowled.

"What are you two up to?" Em asked as she plopped down into Con's lap and kissed the cleft in his chin.

"Just talking. You look beautiful today, Em. Just let me know if this joker ever does you wrong and we can run away together," Jayce said with a grin and Em laughed as Con made a lunge at his friend.

"She looks beautiful every day, Jayce. My wife is the most beautiful woman in this world and ours."

"I totally agree with you!" Lee said as she and Alex sat down. "So, Em. You never did say how you figured out how to defeat the spell the demon was using."

"Well, it was math. The spell was a negative spell, meet a negative with a negative and you get a positive."

"There you are, dear! Congratulations."

Em and Con stood up to greet Adelade Belton, who'd come in from London to attend their wedding.

"Adelade, it's lovely to see you, we're so glad you could make it," Em said as she kissed the other woman's cheeks.

"I wouldn't have missed it for the world. I knew the moment that you two bumped into each other that you were meant to be together."

Con grinned down at Em and kissed her forehead. "Yep, her own personal faerie stalker as she calls me, in what she assures me is affection."

Em gave him a quick grin and allowed him to pull her onto the dance floor and up against his body for a slow number.

"I love you, Conchobar MacNessa," she said with a soft smile.

"I love you too, Emily Charvez, witch of my dreams."

Why an electronic book?

We live in the Information Age—an exciting time in the history of human civilization, in which technology rules supreme and continues to progress in leaps and bounds every minute of every day. For a multitude of reasons, more and more avid literary fans are opting to purchase e-books instead of paper books. The question from those not yet initiated into the world of electronic reading is simply: *Why?*

1. *Price.* An electronic title at Ellora's Cave Publishing and Cerridwen Press runs anywhere from 40% to 75% less than the cover price of the exact same title in paperback format. Why? Basic mathematics and cost. It is less expensive to publish an e-book (no paper and printing, no warehousing and shipping) than it is to publish a paperback, so the savings are passed along to the consumer.

2. *Space.* Running out of room in your house for your books? That is one worry you will never have with electronic books. For a low one-time cost, you can purchase a handheld device specifically designed for e-reading. Many e-readers have large, convenient screens for viewing. Better yet, hundreds of titles can be stored within your new library—on a single microchip. There are a variety of e-readers from different manufacturers. You can also read e-books on your PC or laptop computer. (Please note that Ellora's Cave does not endorse any specific brands.

You can check our websites at www.ellorascave.com or www.cerridwenpress.com for information we make available to new consumers.)

3. *Mobility.* Because your new e-library consists of only a microchip within a small, easily transportable e-reader, your entire cache of books can be taken with you wherever you go.

4. ***Personal Viewing Preferences.*** Are the words you are currently reading too small? Too large? Too… ANNOYING? Paperback books cannot be modified according to personal preferences, but e-books can.

5. ***Instant Gratification.*** Is it the middle of the night and all the bookstores near you are closed? Are you tired of waiting days, sometimes weeks, for bookstores to ship the novels you bought? Ellora's Cave Publishing sells instantaneous downloads twenty-four hours a day, seven days a week, every day of the year. Our webstore is never closed. Our e-book delivery system is 100% automated, meaning your order is filled as soon as you pay for it.

Those are a few of the top reasons why electronic books are replacing paperbacks for many avid readers.

As always, Ellora's Cave and Cerridwen Press welcome your questions and comments. We invite you to email us at Comments@ellorascave.com or write to us directly at Ellora's Cave Publishing Inc., 1056 Home Avenue, Akron, OH 44310-3502.

THE
☥ ELLORA'S CAVE ☥
LIBRARY

Stay up to date with Ellora's Cave Titles in
Print with our Quarterly Catalog.

To recieve a catalog,
send an email with your name
and mailing address to:

CATALOG@ELLORASCAVE.COM
or send a letter or postcard
with your mailing address to:

Catalog Request
c/o Ellora's Cave Publishing, Inc.
1056 Home Avenue
Akron, Ohio 44310-3502